The Black Book
[DIARY OF A TEENAGE STUD]
VOL. I

Girls, Girls, Girls

∎

JONAH BLACK

AVON BOOKS
An Imprint of HarperCollins*Publishers*

The Black Book [Diary of a Teenage Stud], Vol. I:
Girls, Girls, Girls

Copyright © 2001 by 17th Street Productions,
an Alloy Online, Inc. company.

Cover Photograph from Tony Stone
Design by Russell Gordon

Printed in the United States of America.

For information address
HarperCollins Children's Books, a division of
HarperCollins Publishers, 1350 Avenue of the Americas,
New York, NY 10019.

 Produced by 17th Street Productions,
an Alloy Online, Inc. company
33 West 17th Street, New York, NY 10011

Library of Congress Catalog Card Number: 2001116874
ISBN 0-06-440798-5

First Avon edition, 2001

Visit us on the World Wide Web!
www.harperteen.com

Girls, Girls, Girls

—————— ■ ——————

Sophie and I sneak out of her parents' house while everyone is sleeping and we go down to the barn to saddle up the horses. The sunlight is slanting through the windows of the barn, making the spider-webs up near the hayloft glow softly. We saddle up Angel and Blaze and I follow her down the mossy path and soon we are riding along the beach in Maine listening to the sound of the waves crashing against the rocks and the seagulls cawing in the misty sky. The air is cold and the horses' breath comes out in clouds. There is a lobster boat collecting traps out on the water and I can see steam rising from the cup of coffee one of the lobstermen is holding.

"Jonah," Sophie says. "Are you coming?"

I squeeze Blaze's ribs with my heels and we gallop down a path that leads away from the ocean and into the woods. Sunlight shines through the trees and the air smells like pine needles. Ahead of me I can see Sophie's back. Her blond ponytail swings back and forth between her shoulder blades and I can just see the outline of her bra underneath her gray long-sleeved T-shirt. Just above the waistband of her jeans is a patch of bare back, where her shirt has ridden up—the very spot where I am going to kiss her as soon as we get off our horses.

Sophie stops suddenly and turns to look at me. I pull back on the reins.

"What?" I say.

And she says, "Listen."

I stop my horse beside Sophie and reach out to hold her small, perfect hand while we listen to the sound of the woods. There are squirrels chattering and blue jays squawking and the wind is shushing through the pine trees and in the distance the waves thunder against the beach. Sophie is trembling. I have never felt this

Okay, so exactly as I was writing that, this girl bumped my elbow with her hip and she looked at me and said, "Sorry." Then the girl did a double-take and said, "Jonah?" which took me by complete surprise. I mean, I had absolutely no idea who she was. And then she said, "It's me, Luna? Luna Hayes?" And I was like *Are you sure*? because the last time I saw Luna was the end of ninth grade and back then she didn't have hips. From her head to her toes she was just one long skinny thing like a piece of spaghetti. I just sat there in homeroom, staring at her.

"I heard you were coming back!" she said, combing her curly brown hair with her fingers. "You haven't changed at all."

I wasn't sure if not changing in two years was good or bad. In Luna's case, though, changing had definitely been good. Her body was seriously developed now and her face had grown up, too. There was a depth to her eyes that wasn't there before and I wondered if something sad had happened to her. I thought about what Thorne had e-mailed me about Luna, but I never believed it was true.

"Are you okay?" she asked me.

"Yeah, I'm great. It's good to be back in Pompano Beach," I said.

It wasn't a real answer. I mean, am I okay? I'm not really sure. Not as okay as I'd like to be, I guess. But I'm hoping that after today things will be getting more and more okay, because they've been sort of not okay for a while.

"Well, good," Luna said. "I guess things didn't work out in Pennsylvania." She said it, but it was more like a question.

"Not exactly."

"And you're . . ." She was trying to say something but whatever it was she couldn't say it. "Well, I'm glad you're okay. I heard these stories, you know."

"What kind of stories?" I said.

"I don't know." She looked up at the front of the room where our homeroom teacher, Mr. Bond, was reading a thin book called *Howl.* Then she turned back to me. "Well, you look great, Jonah," she said. "Better than I expected."

Gee, thanks, Luna. I mean, it's not like I think I'm hot or anything. I'm tall. In good shape from swimming. My hair is kind of wavy and brown and looks decent, usually. My skin is okay. My eyes are just plain brown, kind of big. I'm all right, I guess. At least I hope so. Anyway, I don't know what Luna was expecting me to look like, but what she said didn't sound like much of a compliment.

"Listen. I'll be sitting over there," Luna said, and then she waved at me like I was somebody driving away in a car.

I turned to look out the classroom window and there was the Atlantic Ocean, twinkling and green in the warm Florida sun. There were speedboats zooming around, and yachts, and way out, a lone sailboat sailed into the horizon.

Sophie turns to me and says in the softest whisper in the world, "I want this moment to last forever."

She leans over and we start to kiss and while we're kissing it begins to rain softly. The forest is humming with the sound of the rain.

"Jonah," Sophie says in that same whisper so soft that I wonder if I'm even hearing it, or maybe I can hear her talking inside my head. "Let's lie down in the moss."

We tie up the horses and sit down on the ground and the moss is softer than velvet; it's like fur. We wrap our arms around each other and lie back and grasshoppers fly out of the moss and up into the air.

"So are you going to remember me, Jonah?" Sophie says, looking into my eyes. She is trembling again, and I hold her tight.

"Yes," I say. "Of course I'll remember you."

"Oh, Jonah. I don't know how I'm going to go on with my normal life after this. It's like, nothing can be put back the way it was."

"But is that what you want? Do you really want everything back the way it was?" I ask her.

"No," Sophie says. She's lying on her back now, looking up at the sky. Tiny raindrops are collecting

on her cheeks. "I just wish it wasn't so complicated. I'm going to miss you so much. I miss you
now, even. It's like you're already gone."

"I'm here."

"I know. But I can't imagine living through next
year, with you back in Florida and me stuck at
Masthead without you."

"You'll be all right," I say, although I kind of like
that she's so upset about me leaving.

"I won't be all right," Sophie says. Her throat
catches and there's that note in her voice that
makes me wonder about her sometimes. Like, if
she's all there, and if she's going to be okay without
someone looking out for her. She starts to cry a little, and she turns her head and smiles at me as if
she's afraid I think she's stupid for crying. Her tears
are made of watery blue ink, staining the collar of
her shirt.

"You'll be okay," I say, stroking her hair.

"It's all my fault," she says. "You getting kicked
out. Having to go back to Florida. Is the school
you're going to anything like Masthead?"

"No, it's just a public high school."

"And what's the town called again?"

"Pompano Beach."

"And what's the point of Pompano Beach again?
Like, what's there?"

I think about Pompano. About Mom and my sister, Honey, and Don Shula High, and my best friends, Thorne Wood and Posie Hoff, and the Intercoastal Waterway, and the beach, and the mall, and I don't know how to explain it. It seems so far away.

"It's the home of the Goodyear Blimp," I say.

"Really?"

"Yeah." I describe the hangar that they keep the blimp in, and Sophie listens, and as she listens the wind blows a pale strand of hair in her eyes. I reach over and fix it, tucking it behind her ear. She wears diamond studs in her ears every day.

For a while we are quiet, listening to the sound of the rain in the tree branches above our heads.

"So what makes it float?" Sophie asks.

"What?" I say.

"The blimp. Is it helium? Or hot air? What is it?" She looks worried. "If it's so easy to get things to float then why aren't there more things up in the air, floating?"

I can tell it isn't really the blimp Sophie's worried about. She looks so distant and troubled, it's like she's the one floating away.

"Sophie," I say. "I will always be

This guy just came over to me and said, "Hey, Jonah." I couldn't believe it. It was Thorne! And he

7

goes, "What are you writing?" and I said, "Nothing," and then I closed the journal. I just sat there staring up at him for a second, and then Thorne whooped and yelled and gave me this big bear hug. I can't believe how much Thorne has changed in two years. He has this little goatee now and he's grown like eight feet. And he acts so different, too. I mean, Thorne was always this gangly geek with braces who couldn't get his zipper to stay up. But now he has this whole aura of coolness and sophistication.

"Jonah, dude," Thorne said, checking me out. "It's like you haven't changed at all!"

This was the second time someone had said this. It was getting annoying.

"You haven't changed, either," I told him, and he just smiled like he knew I was lying.

"You look like you're in good shape, though," Thorne said, smacking my stomach.

"Yeah," I said. "I was on the diving team back at Masthead. I'm going to dive for Don Shula, too, I guess."

"Whoa," Thorne said, "You're like, Mr. Team Spirit!"

I rolled my eyes. "Piss off," I said.

"So what do you think?" Thorne asked, looking around the room like some kind of czar surveying his domain.

I looked around the Zoo, which is what every-body at Don Shula High School calls the senior homeroom. Mr. Bond was sitting at his teacher desk, going through his papers. The rest of the seniors were talking to each other, catching up on the summer. I saw a couple of guys I used to know, including Smacky Platte. Smacky used to be addicted to orange-flavored Tic Tacs and he would sit in the corner chewing on them and playing his Game Boy. Now he has bloodshot eyes and a very stoned-looking perma-grin. It looks like Smacky has some new hobbies.

It was weird, though. The girls had changed even more than the guys. A lot of them I didn't even recognize, and I couldn't tell if it was because they were new or if their bodies and faces had morphed so much that I just couldn't place them. I wish I'd moved back to Pompano in June so I could have caught up with everybody this summer, instead of just dive-bombing in the week school started.

"So what have you heard about Mr. Bond?" I asked Thorne.

Mr. Bond looked kind of retro, with a starched white shirt and a narrow black tie and these thick, black-framed glasses. His black hair was all slicked back and gelled.

—— ■ ——

"Major tight-ass," Thorne whispered back.

I kept looking around for Posie, but I didn't see her anywhere. "Where's Posie?" I said. "I haven't seen her since I got back."

Thorne shrugged. "Posie doesn't do homeroom. She has special permission to come to school an hour late so she can catch the morning waves."

"She's surfing?"

"She's amazing," Thorne said. "A total wahine."

I laughed because I'd forgotten about that word. It wasn't a word I'd heard a lot in Pennsylvania. I guess I've forgotten a lot of things.

"Jesus, Jonah," Thorne said. "It's so completely excellent to have you back. I'm telling you, man, we are going to party this year. Seriously!"

"Sounds good to me," I said.

"So what happened up in Pennsylvania? You got kicked out or something, right?" Thorne asked me.

"Something like that." I really didn't feel like getting into it. "I'll tell you about it later," I said.

This girl with amazing red hair was coming toward us, and suddenly I recognized her. It was Rosemary Mahoney, who I'd known since second grade. Rosemary always got teased for looking like a boy because her mother kept her hair cut short. Now her hair has grown past her shoulders and it's the kind of red that looks natural but it definitely isn't. Rosemary also has the greenest eyes I've ever seen. Maybe they're fake, too.

When she saw me looking at her she said, "Jonah Black! Is that you?" She leaned her head to one side, and her red hair fell like a curtain over one shoulder. "I heard you killed somebody in Pennsylvania. You didn't, did you?"

Right about then Mr. Bond stood up and made a horrible sound writing his name on the blackboard. Rosemary covered her ears with her hands like someone had hit her and then she sat down at a desk right next to me. Then Mr. Bond raised his hands to his face like he was going to shout, but instead he said in this loud, creepy whisper, "Please take your seats, ladies and gentlemen."

We all sat down.

"I am Mr. Bond," he said. We kind of guessed this, because he'd already written his name on the board. "And it is my responsibility to be your home-room teacher for this, your senior year at Don Shula High. It is a responsibility I take seriously. I hope you will value my respect as much as I value yours and we can behave decently toward one another."

Next to me, Thorne leaned back in his chair and pretended to sneeze, saying the word *tight-ass* into his hand.

"Now then," Mr. Bond said. "Ackerman, Dirk?"

This giant mountain of tan muscle, like a two-hundred-pound porterhouse steak, said, "Here." I couldn't believe it. When I left Pompano two years ago, Dirk Ackerman looked like a praying mantis. Steroids. It had to be.

"Ambrasino, Kate?" Mr. Bond said.

"Vanilla," Thorne whispered.

"What?" I whispered back.

"Ambrasino's vanilla. On the Thorne Wood Ice Cream Scale."

"Vanilla? Is that good?" I said.

Thorne nodded, smiling happily. "Vanilla's good."

"Arnold, Christopher?"

Rosemary glances at me sideways and shakes out her red hair. She leans over to whisper to me and I can smell cinnamon and she says, "I don't care if you killed someone. I know it wasn't your fault."

And I say, "I didn't kill anyone, I was just unlucky."

Rosemary looks sad. She pulls a violin out of her backpack and starts to play. It's Chopin, the same piece the guy down the hall from me at Masthead was always practicing. Sophie and I lie on the roof, just looking up at the stars and listening to the sad, faraway music.

"Morrison, Sally?"

"Here."

"Rocky Road," said Thorne.

"Rocky Road?" I said. "Is that better than vanilla?"

"Depends on how you feel about marshmallows," Thorne said.

The music stops, and we lie still. From my roof we can see the moon rising out on the ocean and it's huge and red, like a ball of molten lava. Sophie's skin glows pink in its light, but when I touch her cheek her skin is cold.

"Mint Chocolate Chip," Thorne said about someone, but I didn't catch who.

"Now then," Mr. Bond said, clearing his throat. "Today I would very much like—"

"Hey, Mr. Bond," Thorne yelled out. "You forgot Jonah!"

"Who?" Mr. Bond said, looking startled. I think he was shocked that he had made a mistake. He seemed pretty anal.

I didn't say anything because I was kind of embarrassed. I mean, he'd gotten all the way through the roll and I hadn't even noticed that my name wasn't called.

"Jonah," Thorne said like I was famous or something. "Jonah Black!"

"Who's Jonah Black?" Mr. Bond said impatiently.

A voice said, "I am." And it was me speaking. Everyone stared at me.

"Jonah Black? There's no Jonah Black in this class. Is that really your name?" Mr. Bond said, acting all suspicious.

"Yes," I said. It was really weird, but for a second I wondered if that really was my name. Like, maybe I'm somebody else and I don't even know it. It would be kind of a relief if that were true. But I'm me all right.

"Jonah wasn't here last year," Thorne said, still trying to run interference for me. He sounded like he had everything under control and this would be cleared up in no time. "He was up in Pennsylvania."

"Oh," said Mr. Bond. Suddenly something clicked in his brain, as if he was thinking, *Oh, he's the one.* Then he looked at me, almost sympathetically. "Mr. Black," he said. "I think you'd better talk to Mrs. Perella."

The class groaned. Mrs. Perella, the assistant principal, has a reputation for being a hardass. But Mr. Bond cleared his throat, and the room got quiet again.

"I'd like you to go and speak with Mrs. Perella *right now*, Jonah," Mr. Bond said.

"Okay," I said. I stood up.

"Take your things with you."

"My things?" All of a sudden I got nervous. I couldn't figure out why I should take all my stuff with me if I was just going to sort out some glitch in the system. I'd be right back.

"Yes. Take your things with you," Mr. Bond repeated.

So I picked up my backpack. The room was completely quiet as everyone watched me leave.

The next thing I knew I was in the empty hallway. It smelled like pencil shavings and floor wax and I could hear all the teachers giving their first-day-of-school spiel to their classes.

As I walked down the hall toward the stairwell I heard the pay phone ringing, and I stopped and looked at it. I remember calling Mom on that same phone in the beginning of ninth grade when I'd thrown up right after lunch. The phone is ringing, and nobody is answering it. So I go over and pick it up.

"Hello, Jonah?" she says.

"Sophie?"

"It's me. Listen. I'm naked."

"I can't talk now, Sophie," I tell her. "I think I'm in trouble."

I hung up the phone and walked downstairs, down the long hallway on the second floor to the last office on the left. There was Mrs. Otto, the eight-hundred-year-old secretary to Mrs. Perella and Dr. Chamberlin, the school principal. I think she mostly works for Mrs. Perella, though, because Dr.

Chamberlin is never around. I don't even know what he looks like.

Mrs. Otto looked up and said, "Jonah Black," which was really creepy. I mean, was she expecting me, or did she just remember me from ninth grade?

"Mr. Bond said I should talk to Mrs. Perella," I told her.

"Indeed," Mrs. Otto said. "Have a seat."

I sat down, feeling even more nervous. *Indeed* is never a good word to hear. So I'm writing this while I'm waiting. Mrs. Perella is in her office taking phone calls, mostly from the parents of kids on Bus 13, which is this school bus where fights always break out. Right now, I can hear her saying, "Yes, if you promise to talk to your son. No, we've never had to hire security for any of our other bus routes. All right. Good." Now she's hanging up and

(About twenty minutes later.)

Remain calm, that's the important thing. Freaking out is not going to fix anything.

Too late.

I'm writing this in the cafeteria. There's no one else in here except the lunch ladies frying up burgers for lunch, which isn't for another few hours.

So I finally talked to Mrs. Perella.

She is wearing a green military uniform and she glares at me with her hands in fists and says, "Vee have vays of making you talk!"

And I say, "No. You can torture me, you can kill me, but I don't have to tell you anything!"

She unzips her uniform and pulls a whip out of her leather bustier, which is studded with metal bolts and screws. Then she cracks the whip against her palm and says, "Oh, I zink you vill talk, Jonah. I zink you vill talk very much!"

Mrs. Perella looked up at me as I came into her office and let her Benjamin Franklin glasses slide off of her nose and hang from the gold chain around her neck. There were two red marks on her nose where the nose pads of the glasses had been. She pinched the red places with her thumb and forefinger and closed her eyes, and while her eyes were closed she said, "Jonah."

"Hello, Mrs. Perella," I said. "Mr. Bond said I should talk to you. I wasn't on his attendance sheet."

"Mr. Bond?" she said. "What were you doing in Mr. Bond's class? You're not in Mr. Bond's class, you're in Miss von Esse's class."

"Miss von Esse?" This didn't make any sense because the seniors were all in the Zoo, and there wasn't any place else for me to go, unless they'd put me in the genius section. For that one tiny second I was thinking, *Excellent. If I'm in the genius section I get to sleep an extra half hour in the morning, and ride to school with my sister in her Jeep, and all the colleges are going to love me.* Things were looking up!

"Jonah, you're not in the twelfth grade. You're in eleventh grade. I explained this all to your father," Mrs. Perella said.

I sat there for a moment feeling as if I'd fallen out of an airplane. "Eleventh grade? You're telling me I'm a junior?"

Mrs. Perella took a sip of coffee out of a mug that had a picture of Garfield on the side. "I discussed this matter with your father in some depth. Surely he explained the situation to you?"

"He didn't say anything," I said. Good old Dad. He must have forgotten to mention it. "I'm a junior?"

"I'm afraid so, Jonah. There was a problem with your credits from Masthead Academy."

"But how can I still be a junior?"

Words seemed to fail her for a moment. Then she took a deep breath, gathering her patience. "Jonah, Don Shula is a magnet school. You know that, don't you?" she asked.

I said yes, but I was thinking that this was like one of those car wrecks where everything goes in slow motion.

"Well, I'm afraid that the situation that made it necessary for you to leave Masthead Academy had to be taken into consideration. You did not complete the year in good standing. As a result of the . . . situation."

"The situation?" All I could do was sit there repeating the last thing she'd said.

"Yes. I'm sorry. If you had finished the year with distinction at Masthead, we might have considered matriculating you into the senior class. But our policies are quite clear on this. We can't set a precedent, Jonah. It wouldn't be fair to our other students who have been working with focus."

"Working with focus?" She used all these weird phrases that only high school assistant principals know.

"On their studies. And on their languages in particular. According to your Masthead transcript, you received a D in German last term. That alone was enough to jeopardize your status. But after the—"

"The situation," I said, like a robot.

"Yes. I'm afraid it's out of the question. "

"But I can't be a junior again," I said. "It's not fair!"

Mrs. Perella stood up. "I'm sorry you didn't find out earlier. But I'm sure you will like Miss von Esse's class. She's very popular."

I just sat there staring up at her. I really didn't believe it was true. It couldn't be.

Mrs. Perella sat back down and took a sip of her coffee. "I understand it's been arranged for you to start therapy, Jonah," she said.

I nodded mutely. The jerks at Masthead had suggested to my mom that I see a shrink, and of course Mom thought it was a wonderful idea. My first appointment is tomorrow.

"I hope it helps," Mrs. Perella said. She sipped her coffee again. "Make a nice day, Jonah."

I wanted to hit her. "Make a nice day," I said.

I waited one more second and then this funny look creeps over her face and there's just enough time for her to realize what I've done before the poison I've slipped into the coffee begins to work.

"Jonah," she says, "I'm sorry."

"Oh, I know you are," I say, and she starts to turn blue. "That's extract of Eucalypto. Undetectable. But its effects are powerful."

"Excuse me," she yawns, resting her head on her desk.

"As I'm sure you're aware," I say, "being an educated woman, extract of Eucalypto makes you feel very sleepy. So sleepy you lose control of your faculties."

"Night, night," grunts Mrs. Perella. She wipes her mouth with the back of her hand.

"Wow," I say. "You're drooling. Gross."

I left her office and Mrs. Otto watched me leave and I heard her thinking, *Dead man walking*, and the guards take me by the arms and we walk down a long corridor toward the gas chamber and Thorne and Posie and Luna Hayes and Rosemary Mahoney are all standing there crying. Sophie is on the phone with the governor but she hangs up and shakes her head sadly. I'm brave, I don't cry, I just sit down in the chair they've prepared for me and I say to all my friends, "It's all right. Don't be sad."

I walked up the stairs to the fifth floor and stood in front of the door marked MISS VON ESSE. I could hear the teacher talking to the eleventh graders, and her voice sounded nice. I tried to imagine myself going in and sitting down and everyone staring at me and smirking, but I couldn't do it. So I came down here to the cafeteria and sat down at an empty table and now I'm writing this and I don't know what to

(Still in the cafeteria, but I better make this fast.)

Just as I was writing that, this amazing girl with waist-length golden blond hair walked into the cafeteria. Her hair was wet and she was wearing rubber flip-flops and a short purple sarong skirt that was tied around her waist like a towel. Her legs were tan and wiry and so strong, like a racehorse or something. Beads of water clung to her collarbone, and I could see a red bikini top through her damp white T-shirt.

The minute she saw me the girl stopped and said, "Whoa. Wait. It's not. It's not!"

"Excuse me?" I said.

"It is," she said. "Whoo-hoo! It's Jo-nah!" She dropped all of her stuff on the floor and ran over to me with her arms open and it was then that I realized, it was Posie! I couldn't believe it. I mean, she'd always been cute, but now she is this beautiful, athletic, graceful, sunny *goddess*.

"I can't believe you're here!" she squealed. "Wow!" Her hair smelled like saltwater.

"God, Posie," I said. "You look great!"

"Look who's talking, Jonah! Boy, you haven't changed a bit!"

If one more person says that to me I'm going to go out of my mind.

Posie kind of paused for a second and blinked.

"Wait. What's wrong, Jonah?" she asked me.

"Nothing," I said. It was so like Posie to be able to tell something was wrong with me in less than thirty seconds without me saying anything.

"Bullshit. What's going on? How come you're sitting by yourself in the cafeteria? Isn't first period just about to end?"

I took this huge breath and told her. "You're not going to believe this. They made me a junior. I'm in Miss von Esse's class." I felt sick saying it, like I was making it true.

"No way! They can't do that."

"They say it's because of what happened at Masthead," I said. Of course Posie doesn't know what happened, but I knew that wouldn't matter to her. "I didn't take all of my final exams."

"Oh, that's crap. You know it's crap. Hey, listen. I gotta get to class. But you're going to get out of this mess. I promise. You won't have to be a junior, okay?" She grabbed me and gave me another big hug, making a wet mark on my T-shirt with her hair. "I am so glad you're back. I've got so much to tell you."

"Yeah? You look happy, Posie," I said. She really did. I wish I could feel like she looks—like nothing could go wrong, the world is just this big, wonderful Shangri-la.

"Oh, Jonah, I am happy," Posie said. "I can't wait for you to meet Wailer."

"Wailer? Who's Wailer?"

"My boyfriend. My . . ." She blushed, and I remembered what it's like to see Posie blush. She turns dark purple, like a plum. It's pretty funny, since there isn't too much that makes her blush. I mean, this is a girl who does stuff like chew tobacco, and she was the first person I ever knew to buy a copy of *Penthouse*.

"I want to meet him," I said, but as I said it I realized, I already hate this guy. I mean, what kind of a name is Wailer, anyway?

"You know what he wants to do?" Posie said, so breathlessly she was almost whispering. "He wants us to drop out, get married, go pro. He wants to live on the beach and make babies with me!"

"Whoa," I said. "Hard core." It sounded like the worst idea I had ever heard.

"I know, it sounds insane," Posie said. "But I'm actually thinking about it. I mean, that's how serious it is."

"Wow," I said, wondering what other stuff I'd missed out on while I was gone. "Hey, you want to hang out down at the dune after school?"

"Today's no good," Posie said, and she blushed an even darker shade of purple.

It was pretty clear that she had plans with Wailer after school and those plans were of a sexual nature. I mean, you don't talk about dropping out of high school and marrying someone and living on the beach with them and making babies if you had never had sex with them, right?

So is everyone having sex now? I guess that's something else I missed out on while I was away. Suddenly I am like the lamest person in the entire town.

"How about tomorrow? Is that okay?" Posie offered.

"Okay," I said, trying not to sound disappointed. "I'll see you tomorrow then."

The bell rang. Posie picked up her backpack and ran toward the door. "Welcome back, Jonah!" she yelled as she ran. "We're going to party, okay?"

"Okay, Posie," I said.

So here I am. Probably the only seventeen-year-old virgin in the school and I'm going to stay that way for the rest of my life because why would anyone have sex with someone who had to repeat eleventh grade?

I really have to go check in with Miss von Esse.

But I hear footsteps approaching, and it's Sophie holding this silver platter with two dishes under huge silver domes and a bottle of white wine and two crystal glasses. She sits down next to me and pulls the domes off. There's a lobster on one plate and the book *The Joy of Sex* on the other.

"It's Maine lobster," Sophie says. She opens the bottle of wine and pours it and we ting glasses. Then Sophie pulls one of the lobster's little legs off and sucks on it. I love watching her. She gets butter all over her chin and her eyes shine. "Jonah," she says, pointing at the book. "Will you read to me?"

Outside, the lighthouse beacon flashes, and for a moment we are bathed in bright moving light.

(Later that afternoon. Miss von Esse's classroom.)

Okay, so here I am, in my eleventh grade remedial German class, which turns out to be taught by Miss von Esse in the same classroom as my eleventh grade homeroom, which I missed. When I first came up here to meet Miss von Esse I was thinking, *No way, I can't do this.* When I got to the door, I took a deep breath, kind of pretending I was doing a difficult dive, like a double somersault with a half twist, starting from the handstand position. I execute the dive perfectly and the crowd roars and I plunge into the pool.

"You must be Jonah Black," Miss von Esse said when I opened the door.

I nodded, and she stood up and walked around her desk and handed me my schedule. "I've been waiting for you," she said.

Miss von Esse is preppy, but not in a plain, L.L. Bean sort of way. She's more like the Ralph Lauren model kind of preppy, with straight brown hair that falls just below her chin. A bob, I guess it's called. She looks really young, too. Like, no older than twenty-five. I can picture her in a ski lodge in Vermont at the end of a long day, wearing an Irish fisherman's sweater and her cheeks all red from being on the slopes all day and we're drinking hot mulled wine out of goblets made of red glass. Over by the bar someone is playing Irish folk tunes on the piano and there's a huge fire roaring in the fireplace and above the fire is the head of a stuffed moose with a brass plaque under it that says BAOIGHEOLLEAN.

"I am so glad you are in my class," she says. She leans over my desk and I smell saddle soap. Then Sophie sits down on my lap and takes my face in her hands and kisses me.

"This isn't right," I say. I don't want to do it in a classroom.

But Sophie says, "Let's not worry about right or wrong anymore. Let's worry about what we feel." Then she unbuttons her blouse and hangs it up on the pencil sharpener on the wall. She unhooks her bra and swings it around on the end of her finger, and sways her hips in a dance that reminds me of the Hokey Pokey, only slower.

"I was supposed to be a senior," I whisper to her. "I'm not supposed to be here."

"I know, Jonah," she says, lying back on the satin sheets. "I know."

Ich liebe, du liebst, blah, blah, blah.

Christ. We are actually reviewing the present tense in German right now. I don't believe it. This is my fourth year of German—I'm pretty sure I have the present tense down by now. Seriously, I think I'm going to die.

At lunch, I looked around for Posie and Thorne but of course they have a different lunch period than me because I'm a junior and they are seniors. The only person I saw that I knew was my little sister, Honey, because the senior genius section has the same lunch period as the juniors. Honey is so smart, she got to skip tenth grade, so she's a senior now, which is so unfair I can't even think about it.

She was sitting with all these geeks with oily noses wearing thick glasses and golfing shirts. Honey looks like this rocker chick, not a genius. But that's what's so great about her. She's an enigma.

I walked over to her table. "Hey, Porkchop," she said. "There's a rumor going around you're a junior. Tell me that's bull," she said.

"Oh, it's a big mistake," I lied. "They can't make me repeat eleventh grade, I mean, come on!"

Honey looked me up and down and shook her

head. "You are a junior, aren't you? Boy, is Mom going to be pissed."

"Hey, I want to be the one to tell her," I said. "All right?"

"Whatever," she said, and turned back to this guy sitting next to her, working on some ten-page equation in his notebook. He handed Honey his pencil, and she started filling in numbers really fast with this crazed smile on her face. Honey really gets off on math. It's like a drug for her. Actually, she gets off on everything. Honey is never bored.

"Hey, I'm serious," I said, trying to get her attention back. "You'd think after I'd been gone for like, two years you could at least—"

"Eight hundred and twenty-one days," Honey said, still scribbling in the notebook.

It is so completely insane that she can do that— figure out exactly how many days I've been gone without even trying.

"Yeah. Well, you'd think after all that time that you'd cut me some slack," I said.

Honey looked up as if she was actually noticing me for the first time.

"Listen, Squidly," she said. "Don't worry about it, okay? Mom's so into her stupid book right now, she won't even notice."

"Well, just don't say anything, okay?"

Her eyes narrowed. "Yeah, whatever," she said, and then she went back to scribbling numbers.

I still can't believe my little sister is a senior and I'm a junior. It's like the whole world is upside down. Nothing makes sense anymore.

I sat down at another table and studied my stupid junior class schedule while I ate. Then a girl put her tray down across from me. She had thick curly black hair and she was wearing a lab coat. She was eating ravioli in sauce and she very carefully cut each ravioli in half with her knife and fork. Then she reached into her purse—which was weird because most high school girls don't carry purses, they carry backpacks or courier bags—and she pulled out this container of Kraft Parmesan cheese and shook it on her ravioli. I was thinking, *Oh, my God, she carries her own cheese!* Then she looked up at me and asked if I wanted some cheese and I said yes. So she shook the cheese over my plate.

"I just totally love cheese, don't you?" she asked me. Then she speared her ravioli and chewed it slowly, dabbing the corners of her mouth with her napkin. "Did you know that ravioli means 'pillow' in Italian?" she asked me.

"I didn't know that," I said.

And she said, "Yes. It's so perfect. I mean, I would love to have a ravioli as a pillow."

And I say, "Yes, so would I."

The two of us are lying on a huge, soft bed. The sheets are made of lasagna noodles and the pillows are giant raviolis and all around us is warm tomato sauce and mushrooms. Outside, the chapel bell gongs so I know it's Sunday and Sophie and I can lie there as long as we want to. She's sleeping. I try to reach for her hand, but it's lost in the sauce.

When I looked up, the girl wasn't there anymore, and I looked around but I didn't see her. I looked down at my plate and it was licked clean, but I couldn't remember eating all of my lunch. I wonder if Cheese Girl stole it from me. She was definitely sneaky.

Anyway, I got up and took my tray back and then I went to the bathroom. God, it was like being in a time machine—I mean the bathroom is exactly like it was two years ago. The same stuff scrawled on the walls, the same light blue tile, the same moldy smell. For a second I got so totally overwhelmed I thought I was going to pass out, so I leaned against the wall with my forehead pressing into the cold tiles. Then I heard this voice go, "Hey, man. You okay?"

It was Smacky Platte, in a stall, smoking a cigarette. All I could think was, Smacky the degenerate gets to be a senior, but me, I have to go back to eleventh grade and read *The Color Purple* all over again.

Smacky looked at me and nodded. "You okay, man?"

"I'm fine," I said. I turned on the faucet and started splashing my face with water.

"If you need something to make you feel better, you let me know. No reason to feel down in the dumps," Smacky said, patting me on the shoulder.

"I said I was fine. Jesus Christ!" I growled, shrugging his hand off.

"Yo, man, take it easy. Jesus, man. Mellow out!" Smacky said.

I pull out my badge. "Sorry, Smacky. I'm going to have to take you in."

"Whoa, man, chill!" Smacky says. "This isn't what you think!"

I snap the cuffs on him. "Smacky," I say. "You don't know what I think. Now, are we going to do this the hard way, or should we do it the easy way?"

Then Smacky starts to cry. "Dude," he whimpers. "You gotta believe me."

But I am a rock. I am totally unmoved. "Tell it to the judge, Smacky," I say. I pull out my cell phone and tell the sergeant I'm bringing in another junkie, and the sarge says, "Good work, Jonah, my man. Good work."

(Still Sept. 5, after school.)

When I got home, Honey's Jeep was already in the driveway and Mom was standing in the kitchen, talking on her cell phone. She waved at me and I grabbed a banana and now I'm sitting out on the dock waiting for Mom to get off the phone so I can talk to her about my horrible day. I guess I'm kind of nervous because I just jumped up and down on the dock like it was a diving board and now I've got a splinter in my toe. It hurts like hell.

Okay, I finished the banana. Why can't Mom just get off the phone, already?

Oh, she just waved for me to come into the kitchen. Okay, Sarge. I'm going in.

When I got into the kitchen I realized that Mom was actually on the phone with Mrs. Perella, discussing the whole situation.

"Yes, I understand that," she said. She listened for a moment, tapping her foot impatiently. "Yes," she said. "Yes."

She stopped tapping her foot and started pacing. "But I think you ought to consider your process," she insisted. "All this monkey business sounds like it's about control. You're really not being present to my observations, and it is my son we're talking about, not yours. I'm in a space that's very open and willing to listen, but your space sounds like it's shut tight. You haven't been listening to what I have to say."

I heard furious squawking on the other end.

"Fine," Mom said, sounding like she had stopped caring whether she won the argument or not. "Fine. Thank you."

She hung up.

"Mom . . ." I said.

She held out one hand as if to hold me back, and then she put her other hand on top of her forehead and closed her eyes. She took a deep breath, held it for a moment, then let it out.

"Oh, for heaven's sake," she said. "I need a cup of tea."

"Mom—"

"Jonah," Mom said, her forehead wrinkled with worry. "I just want you to know I'm still proud of you no matter what. You're doing great. You're really trying!"

"Good," I said. "What are you proud of, exactly?"

"Bup, bup," she said, holding out her hand again to stop me from talking. She put her hand on her forehead again and took another deep breath, and held it. While she held her breath, Honey came in. She was wearing this leather thing with studs around her neck that looked kind of like a dog collar. Honey took one look at Mom and rolled her eyes at me.

"You got her doing deep breathing two seconds

after you come inside, Nutly?" Honey said. "You work fast."

Mom exhaled.

"Honey, Jonah hasn't done anything wrong," Mom said. "We need to let him know we're proud of him."

"For what?" Honey said.

"For dealing so well with his needs and his situation."

"What needs?" Honey said.

"What situation?" I said.

Mom patted her hair, which is now dyed a sort of beige color and styled like a newscaster's. Camera ready. She put the kettle on the stove and got out a box of Female Toner tea. The box looked pretty beat up.

"You'd think a boy who has to repeat eleventh grade all over again would be depressed," Mom said proudly.

"You sure would!" Honey chimed in.

"But look how well Jonah's doing," Mom said. "He's smiling!"

I was only smiling because I didn't know what other face to make. I had kind of forgotten what a freak my mother is.

"Jonah," Mom said, talking very slowly. "I just got off the phone with Mrs. Perella. She confirmed what Honey told me. You're repeating junior year."

I glared at Honey. "You told Mom already?"

Honey went to the pantry and got out a box of Ring Dings. "Yeah," she said. "It seemed like the right thing to do." She unwrapped a Ring Ding and stuffed it into her mouth whole. "Hey, Ma, can I have some whiskey?" she said when she'd swallowed it.

"No. Have an apple or a cheese stick."

"Aw, you never let me do anything!" Honey said. She grabbed the keys to her Jeep.

"Where are you going, Pumpkin?" Mom said.

"I'm meeting the football team," Honey said.

"Really?" said Mom. "Are you helping them with their homework?"

Honey gave me this big smile. "Yeah, that's what I'm doing," she said. "I'm helping them with their homework." Then she winked at me and left.

"She's so thoughtful," Mom said.

"Yeah, I guess that's one word for it," I said.

"Jonah, I know you must have a lot of feelings right now," Mom said. "If you want to talk you know I'm always here. And you have your first session with your therapist tomorrow, which is going to do wonders for you. But . . ."

She got down a well-worn copy of her new best-selling book. On the front was the title, orange letters against a black background: *Hello Penis! Hello Vagina!*

"I think this will help, too," she said. "Try chapter eight, 'Exploring the Forbidden.'"

Mom thinks all problems in life have something to do with the way you deal with sex when you're a teenager. She's so fanatical about it, she wrote that book, which I haven't read. I'm not going to, either.

"Mom, I don't have a problem—"

"Bup, bup," she said, holding out her hand again, and putting the other hand on her forehead. Big inhale, big exhale.

Her cell phone rang, and she whisked it off the table. "Hello?" she said. "This is she."

She put one hand over the receiver. "I have to take this," she told me. Then she walked outside with the phone and sat down by the pool, and I walked into my room, and lay down on the bed.

While I was away, Mom remade my room into a guest bedroom. It has mint-green wall-to-wall carpeting and a matching mint-green bedspread. There's a little table next to the double bed with a dinky little lamp and a box of Kleenex. There's nothing on the walls except a framed print of a sailboat over the bed. It looks like a motel room.

How appropriate.

About five minutes later, Mom came back and knocked on my door. I said, "Yeah?"

Mom came in. "Good news, Jonah." She looked

very excited. I sat up, all happy, thinking, *Mom talked to the school board. They worked something out. I'm a senior again!*

"Guess whose radio show is going national?" she said.

"Guess whose . . . what?"

"That was my agent. They closed the deal. My radio show is syndicated, coast to coast! *Pillow Talk*, they're calling it, with Dr. Judith Black. Oh, Jonah, this is what we've always wanted!" She hugged me.

"They know you're not a doctor, though, right?" I said.

Mom looked at me, all hurt. "Well, that wasn't a very empowering thing to say."

"Mom," I said. "It's just that people are going to call you up with their, you know—"

"With their sex problems?"

"Yeah, and they're probably thinking you're a doctor. Which you're not. Does that seem right?"

"Jonah," Mom said suspiciously. "Are we play-ing the Honesty Game?"

"I'm just asking a question," I said.

"It's a stage name, Jonah. Like Marilyn Monroe was really named Norma Jean. And Judy Garland was named . . . something else."

"So Doctor isn't a title? It's like, your first name?" I asked, laughing at how ridiculous this sounded.

"Like some people are called Mary Lou or Kathy Jo, but you're called Doctor Judith? Is that it?"

But my mother didn't think this was funny at all. She takes herself pretty seriously.

"Jonah," Mom said angrily. "This is a big thing for our family. This means money. An income. So I can pay for Honey's college." She looked out at the pool, all misty-eyed. "And your college, too," she said, like an afterthought.

"Sorry, Mom," I said. "I'm glad for you. It's good news. Really."

"It's not easy raising two children all by yourself! Your father doesn't do anything! I have to get by on my own!"

I had a choice here. I could point out that, in fact, our fairly well-off dad still pays all our bills and is definitely paying for our colleges. But I decided not to say anything.

"I know, Mom," I said. "I'm sorry. I really am happy for you."

"Are you?" Mom said, all earnest. "Really?"

Her cell phone rang again and she flipped it open. "Hello?" She put her hand over the receiver. "I have to take this," she told me. Then she got up and walked down the hall to her bedroom and shut the door.

Wow, it's great to be back.

Sept. 6

I'm sitting in First Amendment Pizza, waiting to talk to Mr. Swede about getting my old job back. It's very busy in here so I guess I'm going to have to wait awhile. Anyway, school today kind of sucked, but what's new? All day long all I thought about was how I can get out of the eleventh grade and back into the senior class. I think I'm going to write some letters to the school board maybe, or the governor if I have to. I'm not staying in eleventh grade, that's for sure.

After school I had to go down to Amerishrinks at the Pompano Square Mall for my first meeting with the shrink.

I don't know what to think about Dr. LaRue. I mean, what kind of shrink has an office in a shopping mall, anyway? It's like a chain therapy franchise, I guess, because in the waiting room there was this pamphlet that said, *"Visit our other fifteen locations in central Florida."* So if you start to flip out while you're on the highway, you can always pull into one of these Amerishrinks outlets. How reassuring.

There was this girl a year or two younger than me sitting in the waiting room, reading a copy of *Glamour*. Her hands were so small they looked like little bear paws. She glanced up at me, and then quickly looked back down at her magazine. On the cover of the magazine were the titles of all these articles, like *30 Sex Secrets*, and *Look Good Naked,* and I tried to guess which one she was reading. The girl heaved this big, exhausted sigh. I wondered if she was waiting to see the same shrink as me, and what her problem was.

Then she starts to sniffle and I see that she's crying. She puts down the magazine, which is open to an article titled *30 Ways to Have Sex with Jonah.*

"Are you here to see Dr. LaRue?" I ask her.

"Yes," she says. "And I am so afraid."

"What are you afraid of?" I ask.

And she says with this sudden flood of tears, "Oh, I'm afraid of you, Jonah. I'm afraid you don't love me!"

I go over and sit down next to her and hold her hand. She's wearing an Indian bead bracelet that doesn't really go with her diamond stud earrings.

"Sophie, you don't have to worry about anything anymore," I say.

And she says, "It's hard to let go of your fear when you've been afraid all your life."

"You don't have to be afraid from now on," I tell her. She closes her eyes and her lips part softly and I kiss her and her lips taste like saltwater.

The girl's mother came out a moment later. She weighed like three hundred thousand pounds and she said in this gravelly voice, "Come on, Crystal, let's go."

The girl kind of shrank into herself, and I understood what she had been so sad about. She wasn't sad because she had to have therapy; she was sad because she hated her mother.

Then Dr. LaRue said, "Come on in, Jonah."

I got up and went into Dr. LaRue's office. It wasn't a very nice office. There were fluorescent lights overhead that buzzed and the floor was dirty gray linoleum, like an airport bathroom. The walls were papered with blue and white stripes and a framed diploma from the University of Central Florida was hanging from a hook on the back of the door.

Dr. LaRue was sitting behind a messy metal

desk. He's a small man, about fifty, with a bald head and a tiny toothbrush mustache. He reminded me of that Muppet on *Sesame Street* who is always being tortured by Grover.

"Hello, Jonah," Dr. LaRue said. "I'm Dr. LaRue, but if you prefer you can call me Lenny."

"Hi, Dr. LaRue," I said. I sat down in the big blue armchair in front of his desk.

He waited for me to say something more, but I didn't.

"Jonah, your mother is very concerned about you. That's why she asked me to see you. Do you think your mother has reason to be concerned?"

"I don't know." What was I supposed to do? Just tell him the whole story of my life?

"You just moved back to Pompano Beach after living in Pennsylvania for two years. How does it feel to be back?"

"I don't know. All right, I guess." I could already see that therapy was going to be a big waste of time.

"And it's my understanding that you were attending a private boarding school up there? A place called Masthead Academy?"

"Yes. I was at Masthead."

"Were you sad about being asked to leave Masthead?"

"Sad? Um, yeah. I guess I was sad. Sure." What a great diagnosis doctor: Jonah, you are sad.

"Why were you sad?"

"Because they asked me to leave?"

"And why did they ask you to leave?"

"I don't know," I said.

Actually, I don't really know. I mean they could have just suspended me, or made me repeat junior year *there*, or something. I don't know why they had to kick me out. Maybe they didn't want to be responsible if I did something really dangerous.

"Jonah, did your getting kicked out have anything to do with girls' underwear?"

He sat there, very wound up, fingering his little mustache. Suddenly I started laughing. I felt bad, but I couldn't stop. It was all too ridiculous.

"Did I say something funny, Jonah?" he asked me.

I tried to answer but it was impossible. I wiped the tears from my eyes and Dr. LaRue handed me a box of tissues. "It's all right, Jonah. There are a lot of men who like to wear women's underthings. There is nothing wrong with it."

I made myself stop laughing.

"No, it's not that," I said, trying to be serious. "Is that really what they told you? That I like to wear—?"

"Well, I was given to understand by your mother—"

"Dr. LaRue, I may have a lot of problems, but wearing girls' underwear isn't one of them. Mom tends to exaggerate," I told him.

There was a long silence. I think Dr. LaRue was embarrassed. His left leg was bouncing up and down nervously. I don't think he even knew he was doing it.

"So what *are* your problems, Jonah?" he said. "Do you want to talk about them?"

"My problems?"

"Yes. You said you have a lot of problems. What are they?"

I looked at the clock. "How much time have we got?"

Dr. LaRue shrugged. "Enough to get started."

"Well, okay," I said.

"All right then. Tell me," he said.

I opened my mouth but nothing came out, so I shut it again. I tried to think back to when everything in my life started going wrong, but I couldn't think of a good starting point. Was it when I got kicked out of Masthead, or when I first saw Sophie, or way before that? Was it when I first left Florida two years ago to live with Dad? Or when my parents got divorced? Or maybe it was when I was still in the womb, this little bundle of cells, all pissed off about the way my mom's amniotic fluid tasted.

Dr. LaRue blew the air through his lips, making a sound like a horse. I guess he was getting impatient.

Sophie sits down on Dr. LaRue's desk. She is wearing brown suede chaps over her cutoffs. She smells like hay and Murphy's Oil Soap.

"Are you going to tell him?" she asks me.

I don't answer. I still can't figure out where to begin.

"Jonah?" said Dr. LaRue.

"I'm thinking," I said.

"Jonah, don't tell him," Sophie says.

I heard the clock ticking and the sound of people talking in the dentist's office on the other side of the wall.

Sophie just sits there, perched on the edge of the desk, waiting for me to say something.

But I never did. Dr. LaRue stood up and told me time was up. I'd wasted the whole hour.

I guess I was pretty depressed after I left his office. I was supposed to meet Posie and Thorne down at the dune where we always used to hang out and I wasn't really up for it anymore. But I figured if anybody was going to understand it would be those guys.

It took about fifteen minutes to ride over to the ocean. The dune seemed smaller to me than it had in ninth grade. Back then it always seemed like this big hill of sand overlooking the ocean. But when I locked up my bike and started walking toward the beach all I could think was, *That's it*? I wondered if there had been some kind of hurricane that had blown most of the old dune away. Then I realized that it just *seemed* smaller now. In a way, everything does. Well, maybe not smaller, but not as good.

Thorne and Posie weren't the only ones at the dune. There were two other people there with them, a girl and a guy I'd never seen before. And there were a bunch of people sitting around on the beach nearby, watching the surfers and hanging out.

When he saw me Thorne called out, "Hey, Jonah's here!" And Posie let out this loud whooping sound. Everyone on the dune turned to look at me.

Posie was sitting with this guy who I knew right away was Wailer. He was big and muscular with a white triangle of zinc oxide on his nose and this leather string with a shark tooth on it tied around his neck. They were holding hands, and when I walked up to them Posie said, "Wailer, this is Jonah, the first love of my life."

I blushed even though what Posie said isn't true. We've always been just friends. Wailer laughed and shook my hand like he knew Posie was joking. That pissed me off. I mean, what if I really was her first love?

Thorne had his arm around this girl I didn't recognize.

"This is Jonah Black," he said. "Jonah, this is Lucy." Then I remembered who she was: Lucy McIntyre, who used to be this chubby short girl who lived in a modern glass house with two St. Bernards named Genius and Stupid. In grade school Lucy always had big birthday parties out by her pool and those huge dogs would knock kids over and drool all over them and make them cry. Lucy is still short, but the only chubby part of her now is her chest.

"Hi, Jonah," Lucy said. "Wow, you haven't changed a bit."

Everyone keeps saying this and it's driving me crazy. Does this mean I still look like a ninth grader? Bullshit.

"So you surf, Jonah?" Wailer asked.

"No," I said. "Never got into it."

Wailer laughed and shook his head like that was funny. "Dude never got into it," he said to himself. It was like he was saying, *This guy's a total moron.*

"Jonah just got back from his psychiatrist," Thorne announced, like this was something cool that everyone should know. They all looked at me.

"You going to Amerishrinks?" said Lucy. She acted like everybody went there.

"Yeah," I said.

"Isn't Dr. LaRue the best?" Lucy said, letting her head fall back and giggling. "He's such a hottie!"

Yeah, right, I thought. Dr. LaRue sure is sexy.

I think Posie sort of read my mind. "Lucy thinks all doctors are hotties," she said.

"Oh, come on. That little mustache? The way he's always snorting and stamping his feet like a big old horse?" Lucy giggled again. "Wouldn't you love to do it with Dr. LaRue? Just tickle him and melt him like a stick of butter? I would!"

I couldn't believe the way she was talking. But Thorne seemed to be getting off on it.

"Hey, you can tickle me anytime," he said.

"So is everyone here like, seeing a shrink?" Wailer asked. He didn't sound happy about it.

"Oh, Wailer," Posie said. "Everybody goes to Dr. LaRue!" She winked at me.

Wailer's mouth dropped open. "Thorne, you ever seen this guy?"

"Yeah, me, seeing a shrink!" Thorne said, like it was totally impossible. "I don't *think* so!"

Wailer nodded. "Dude," Wailer said. "We're the only ones here who aren't mental!"

"How crazy is that?" Thorne said, shaking his head.

"Oh, Thorne, don't feel left out," Posie said. "You're more screwed up than anybody."

"Thank you," Thorne said, smiling happily.

"Hey, Wailer," Posie said. "Let's get back in the water." She picked up her board and looked out at the ocean like it was a big bowl of ice cream she couldn't wait to eat. Wailer looked at Posie with pretty much the same expression.

"Later, Jonah," Posie said, and they both ran down the beach and jumped into the surf.

We sat and watched them for a while and seriously, they're the best surfers I've ever seen. Posie looks like a superhero when she's surfing. She just glides across the water like it's nothing, with this beautiful smile on her face and her hair flying out behind her. It's unbelievable.

"So, Thorne," I said after a while. "How are your parents? Are they still running the motel?"

"Yeah," Thorne said. "But Pop is branching out. He's got a new business, taking tourists out on a catamaran. You know, sunset cruises and bachelorette parties. Stuff like that."

"How's the house? Did they get the porch done ever?"

"Oh, we moved," Thorne said. "We're down by the cemetery now."

"Thorne won't have me over to his house," Lucy said to me.

"It's being remodeled," Thorne said. "I'll have everybody over when the place is fixed up."

"I think he's lying," Lucy said, pinching Thorne's arm. "Doesn't it sound like he's lying?" she asked me.

"Hey," Thorne said, "if you can't trust me, who can you trust?" And the way he said it made me think maybe he really was lying.

Lucy rolled her eyes and looked at me like I was the only other person in the world who knew how full of it Thorne was. She was wearing big gold hoop earrings that swung back and forth.

"So, Jonah," Thorne said. "Are you ever going to tell me why you got kicked out of boarding school, or am I going to have to torture it out of you?"

"Give me a break," I said.

"Well, how about like, a general idea. Like, you flunked out? Or your pops didn't pay the tuition? Or they caught you smoking crack?"

"I heard there was a fire," Lucy said, quietly. She started twisting her short brown hair around her index finger and I couldn't stop watching her. It was like she was knitting. "I heard you almost died."

It was kind of strange that Lucy said she'd heard there was a fire because on my last night at Masthead I went down to the train tracks, which was the only place I could get any privacy, and burned my old journals. I stood there watching them go up in smoke and just looked at the pages as they turned brown. It was sad how fast they disintegrated. Two years of my life, just ashes in only a few minutes. I started keeping a journal when I went away to boarding school. I was waiting for my plane to Pennsylvania, and I went into the news shop at the airport and saw this blank book and I thought it was cool. So I started writing that day, and I never stopped. I filled five blank books up in two years. But after everything that happened, I didn't want to risk people reading them, so I burned them.

I stand by the tracks just staring at this sad pile of ashes and then I hear sirens and the fire department rushes up in their trucks and the firefighters jump out in their black coats and yellow hats and one of them comes up to me and says, "Jonah, is everything okay?"

"Sophie," I say, "it's done. They're all destroyed."

And she says, "Are you positive?"

And I say, "Yes, don't worry; no one will ever find out."

"Good," she says. Then she reaches her arms out to me and as she does the front of her fire coat falls open and she isn't wearing anything underneath. The wind is blowing smoke in our faces and she wraps me in her coat and I kiss her over and over.

"Jonah?" Thorne said, kicking sand at me.

"I don't want to talk about it," I said in a voice that basically meant, *Leave me alone*.

Nobody said anything for a while. Then Lucy stood up and said she had to head home and she walked back up the beach to the parking lot. Thorne and I just sat there watching Posie and Wailer out on the waves.

"They're pretty serious, aren't they?" I asked Thorne.

"Wailer and the Hoffster? Yeah, they're serious, all right. It's so lame," he said.

"But they look good together," I said.

"Yeah, well, I'll remind you you said that," Thorne said, shaking his head. "If you ask me, he's ruined her."

I was glad to hear that Thorne doesn't like Wailer, either. Thorne's pretty perceptive, come to think of it, even though these days he acts like this cool dude who doesn't think about anything but sex.

We sat there for a while. Then Thorne said, "So you're a junior? Is that like, permanent?"

"No way," I said. "It's a mistake."

"It better be," Thorne said. "The juniors suck."

After a while Wailer and Posie came in and dried off, and Thorne gave Wailer a ride home in his Beetle. That left Posie and me sitting there, watching the ocean.

"I'm glad you're back," she said. "It seems like you've been gone forever."

"Two years," I said.

"It feels like longer than that," Posie said.

Posie and I never really talked while I was away. I talked to Thorne all the time on e-mail, but Posie doesn't like e-mail. She wrote me four letters on this blue whale writing paper I gave her for her birthday when she was ten. One time, she sent me this big piece of dead skin from a blister on her heel. She Scotch-taped it to the letter and drew an arrow pointing to it and underneath the arrow she wrote, "My blister." I guess it sounds kind of gross, but I just thought it was funny. I still have the letters.

Posie rested her elbows on her knees and looked out at the surf. Her skin was glistening with tiny beads of water.

"The waves are perfect today," she said. "Did you see how I dropped into that barrel? It was awesome."

"You looked great," I said. "I never knew you could surf like that."

"I love surfing with Wailer," Posie said. "It's like connecting with someone on a whole other level."

"Uh-huh," I said. What else could I say?

"Oh, Jonah," Posie said, turning to me. Her nose was running and her eyelashes were wet. She looked beautiful. "I think I'm totally in love!"

It was hard to be excited for her. I just kind of smiled.

She started poking at the sand with a little coffee stirrer that was lying around. "So why won't you tell anybody about what happened up at boarding school?" she asked me.

"It's not that I *won't* tell anybody," I said. "It's just . . . complicated."

"You don't have to tell me," Posie said. "But I'm around if you want to talk, or whatever. You know that, right?"

I was watching Posie's wrist as she flicked the sand around with the coffee stirrer. Her wrist bones are so pronounced and sturdy-looking. And yet her arms are covered with fine blond baby hairs. She's a paradox.

Posie punched me in the arm, hard. "I said, *right*?"

"Right," I answered, although I couldn't remember what we were talking about.

"Maybe I'll come by one of these nights in the outboard and we can buzz up the Intercoastal. I'll do it just like I used to, okay? I'll tie up the boat on your dock and knock on the glass door outside your room. Nobody even has to know."

"All right," I said.

Posie looked at her watch. "Hey, I just want to catch a few more waves before sunset. You don't mind, do you, Jonah?"

I shrugged. "Nah, I better go anyway," I said.

Posie jumped to her feet. "I'm really glad you're back!" she said.

She bent down and kissed me on the cheek and her wet breasts pressed into my shoulder. Then she ran down the beach with her board and flopped into the waves on her stomach. I looked down and there were two round wet marks on my shirt.

I was glad I was back, too.

I got up and got my bike and walked with it down the beach for a while, thinking about everything that had happened in the last couple of days.

I'm not sure I can write down exactly what I was thinking. It was just a mix of stuff. First I was feeling really happy. Then I started thinking about Posie and Wailer and Thorne and Lucy and whoever else is Thorne's favorite flavor of ice cream or whatever, and then I got kind of depressed and lonely. I was thinking about how Posie said she was in love with Wailer and how it didn't seem real somehow. And then I started thinking about love in general and wondering if it isn't all just a bunch of crap. I mean, Mom and Dad said they loved each other, and now Dad lives in Pennsylvania with Tiffany and Mom is here in Pompano talking about sex on public radio.

So I walked down the beach thinking all sorts of screwed-up thoughts like that and getting more and more down. After a while I got to the old lifeguard stand and I climbed up and watched the sun set. The beach was deserted. There was a sign on the side of the tower written in chalk: OCEAN TEMP: 68. WINDS: 15 MPH. WARNING. MAN-OF-WAR. RIPTIDES. UNDERTOWS. I could still see Posie out on the ocean, surfing. She looked so relaxed and alive out there. She looked like she belonged.

At that moment this old guy suddenly climbed up the tower and sat down next to me. He must have been about eighty. He pulled out a cigar and lit it and blew a big cloud of smoke out toward the sea.

"She's a peach, isn't she?" he said.

"Who?" I said.

He pointed at the water with his lit cigar. It had a band of paper on it that said CORONA NEGRO. "The mopsytop."

He blew another cloud of smoke. It was blue.

"I tell you," he said. "Girl like that'll make you wanna walk the doggie!"

He laughed like this was the funniest thing he'd ever said. I looked at him like he was insane.

"Don't look at me like that, Chipper. It's what we're here for."

"What?"

He leaned toward me.

"To love women!"

I just nodded. He seemed pretty harmless.

"Name's Pops Berman. I live over there."

He pointed with his cigar toward the big condo building called Niagara Towers. He shook his head. "Viagra Towers," he said sadly.

"You're retired?" I asked.

"Hell, you gotta be retired to live there. You got a pulse, they don't let you in."

"I'm Jonah Black," I said.

He tipped his baseball cap. It was a Red Sox cap, red with a fancy *B*. "Hello, Jonah Black."

I liked Pops. His voice was deep and crinkly and full of experience. But he seemed like kind of a joker, too. And his breath smelled like peanut butter.

He looked out at Posie surfing.

"It's a world full of miracles," he said. "A world with women in it. What do you think about their incredible cabooses, Jonah Black? Don't you love their incredible cabooses?"

Pops kind of shouted when he talked, like Regis Philbin. I looked at my watch. "I gotta go," I said. I stood up.

"I'm not crazy," he said. "I'm telling you God's truth. Is there anything in the world like them?"

"Like what?"

"Women's arses! Unbelievable!"

"I guess," I said. I started to leave.

"Okay, Chipper. You remember what I said then," Pops said.

"Okay. About what?"

"About why we're here."

"Which was what again?"

He shook his head, disappointed in me.

"Women! To love women!" he shouted.

"Okay."

I climbed down the ladder and wheeled my bike up to the road. Behind me I could hear Pops singing on top of the lifeguard tower: "'Hello young lovers, wherever you are. . . . I've had a love like yours. . . .'"

I pedaled north, past all the beach motels and the seedy condo developments. The wind was gusting and the palm trees were rustling and I saw a coconut fall out of a tree and shatter on the blacktop of A1A.

I thought about what Pops had said.

I don't know if I want to love all women, but it might be nice to love one. And to have her love me back.

"But I do love you," Sophie says, pulling up next to me on her mountain bike. "Don't you know that by now?"

"I know," I tell her. Then she waves and bikes off way into the distance.

I can't keep up with her. She's fast.

I wrote that whole last part while I was waiting to see the Swedes about my job. Now I'm back home, sitting on the dock in the dark, watching the yachts go by on Cocoabutter Creek. I wish we had a yacht.

After I left the beach I rode around Pompano for a while, and eventually wound up at First Amendment Pizza. I sat there for almost an hour, writing in my journal, waiting until things calmed down. Finally Mr. Swede came over to talk to me.

"Yonah!" he said, like I was his long-lost son. "Yonah Black!"

Mrs. Swede dropped her pizza paddle on the floor. I guess she hadn't noticed me sitting there all that time.

"It isn't him!" she said.

"It's him," Mr. Swede said.

"It's me," I said.

"Yonah," said Mr. Swede. He took off his apron and hugged me. Mrs. Swede waited till he was done, and then she hugged me, too. Being hugged by her is like sitting down in a big old armchair with all the stuffing falling out of it.

"I wanted to ask you if maybe—"

"Yes," said Mrs. Swede.

"Of course," said Mr. Swede.

"I'm back for good now so I was wondering if I could start—"

"You vant to get back to vork, you get back to vork. Here," Mr. Swede said. He handed me three boxed-up pizzas and two videos. "You make delivery. First day back at vork! Zings go better now! Yonah Black, back on yob!"

"But how much am I going to get p—"

"Ve vork dat out," said Mr. Swede.

"Make delivery," said Mrs. Swede. "Talk later."

So, just like old times, I was back on my bicycle, delivering pepperoni pizzas and rental movies around Pompano.

It's weird. Sometimes I feel like my life takes care of itself. I mean, everything just *happens*, and I go along for the ride. I don't feel like I'm making any choices, I'm just living kind of *accidentally*. I wonder if anyone else feels like this, or if I'm crazy.

Anyway, the first delivery I had to make was down in Cypress Cove to this guy named Sawyer. So I went west on Tenth as far as the water treatment plant, then south on Fifth Avenue and across

Atlantic on Cypress. I leaned my bike against a palm tree and went up to the door with a pepperoni-and-green-pepper pizza and a movie called *Sorority Catfight*, which I've never seen. Sounds pretty dirty, though.

Mr. Sawyer opened the door like two seconds after I rang the bell. He was wearing a white shirt and a blue tie and his boxer shorts. It looked like he came home from work, took off his coat and his pants, and dialed First Amendment and ordered *Sorority Catfight* and then sat there drinking a gin and tonic until I showed up. He looked like the kind of guy who'd give you your driver's test at the DMV. Which I actually need to take again, soon. But that's another story.

Mr. Sawyer handed me twenty bucks and said, "Keep the change," which was a five-dollar tip, so he wasn't all bad. I took the twenty and he closed the door and while I biked away I could imagine Mr. Sawyer eating pepperoni and watching the girls from Delta Thigh Delta have a pillow fight.

Next I rode south to McNab and over to the High Ridge Estates. This was a big, two-story, million-dollar house. There was a Volkswagen Jetta in the driveway, which didn't seem to go with the fancy house. They had ordered *Titanic*, but no pizza.

I rang the bell and a girl came to the door. I held up the videos and said, "Video guy." She smiled and then I realized, it was Cheese Girl from the school cafeteria!

She took the tape from me. "Wait here a sec and I'll get the money," she said. She left me there without inviting me in, so I had to stand in the doorway looking down the hall at this crazy blue cuckoo clock. Then she came back and gave me ten bucks.

"Keep the change," she said.

The movie only cost $3.99 to rent. "Are you sure?" I asked.

"Sure. I stole the money from my mother, anyway. She'd hit the roof if she found out I was renting it again. I've seen it like a hundred times already." She looked at me with huge brown eyes. "Have you seen it?" she asked.

"Yeah," I said. "I've seen it."

"Isn't it just the saddest movie ever? I love it!"

"It is sad," I said.

Actually the first time I ever saw *Titanic* it really made me angry. I mean, like fifteen hundred people die and they have to make up some junk about a missing necklace in order to make it dramatic? But then I saw it a second time recently, when it was on TV, and I liked it. It's kind of haunting, I guess. I

— ■ —

really like that scene when Leonardo Whatshisface is drawing the girl nude and the two of them are looking at each other, really looking, and they forget to be embarrassed.

Cheese Girl licked her lips. She was wearing that kind of lipstick girls wear that makes it look like they're not wearing any lipstick, their lips are just really shiny. Lip gloss.

"I saw you at school yesterday, remember? I'm Donna Mannocchi," she said.

"Yeah, I remember," I said.

"You're Jonah Black, aren't you?"

"Yeah."

She smiled, but she looked sort of nervous. "So like, are you okay?" she asked.

"Yeah." I said. "Why do you ask?"

"I don't know," she said. "I've heard some stories."

"Like what kind of stories?" I don't know where everyone's getting this stuff from, but they are making my life sound so much more dramatic than it really is.

"And you were in some sort of trance at lunch yesterday. I started talking to you and it was like I wasn't even there," Donna said.

"You were talking to me?"

She nodded. "Listen," she said. "I want you to know, there's nothing wrong with it. Lots of people are on it."

"On what?" I had no idea what she was talking about.

"Medication. I used to be on Xanax and now I'm on Paxil. It's not a big deal. It really helps."

At that moment I felt like *I* was on drugs.

"Thanks," I said. I couldn't think of anything else to say.

"So you were at boarding school?" Donna asked.

"Yeah," I said. "Masthead Academy."

"And you were in some car accident? Is that right? And your girlfriend . . . got killed?"

"What?" I said. "Is that what people think?" I noticed the smallest blob of tomato sauce in the corner of Donna's mouth. Had it been there since lunch? I wondered. Or had she come home and had more pasta? I imagined her sitting at her kitchen table, reading *Seventeen*, and eating this big bowl of spaghetti. Cheese Girl is starting to be one of my favorite people in the entire world.

The phone started ringing. "I have to go," she said, giving me the money. "But listen. There's this big party in a couple of weeks," she said. "At Luna's. Are you going?"

Of course I didn't even know there was a party at Luna's. As usual, I'm the last one to find out about everything.

"I don't know," I said. "Are you?"

"Yeah, I'll probably go. Maybe I'll see you there, okay?"

"Okay. Maybe I'll see you."

Cheese Girl closed the door and I got on my bike and rode away. Then this voice calls after me, *Jonah, come back, I made sauce.* I'm thinking, no, don't go back. It's a trap. But then she calls again: *I need help. Will you help me, Jonah?*

So I ride back up her driveway and my wheels crunch the autumn leaves on the black tar. Inside the art studio I can see Sophie, making dough. Her arms glisten with olive oil up to her elbows as she mixes the flour and eggs in the bowl with her hands. She pulls my hands into the bowl, and together we knead the warm, soft dough. On the stove is a cauldron of steaming water, and the whole room is damp and hot, like a steam bath. Sophie stirs the sauce with a long wooden spoon and the air smells like basil and parsley and tomatoes and garlic. She holds out the spoon for me to taste it and looks up at me with sparkling, speaking eyes. "Do you like it?" she says.

(Still Sept. 6, almost midnight.)

I'm lying in bed but I can't sleep. I wanted to write about the bicycle ride home from First Amendment Pizza tonight after dark, because for the first time since I got back I felt like this really is my home.

It was a beautiful night and the stars were all out. I rode through Avalon Gardens over to Highway 1 and stopped in the middle of the road to look at the miles of green lights going yellow and then red, a straight flat line all the way to Ft. Lauderdale. Then I rode past the Pompano Square Mall, and the Muvico 18 theater, and the Wendy's, and the Evinrude dealers, and the closed-up bar with a sign that said GIRLS GIRLS GIRLS, and the Deadhead shop, and the Frank N' Stein, and the Sears.

I cut through Cresthaven, past all the houses that look exactly the same. All the houses are all so close together here, even where the millionaires live, up in Hillsboro and Deerfield and Lighthouse Point. You'd think if you paid millions for your house you'd at least get some privacy. I guess that's a real difference from Pennsylvania, where if you have a million-dollar house you probably have a pretty big lawn.

From Cresthaven I rode into the public park, past the airport and the Goodyear Blimp Base. The Blimp was sitting in the hangar with all the lights on, and there were men swarming around it like worker ants servicing the queen. I went past the dump and the water treatment plant and the public hoops court where Thorne and Posie and I used to play sometimes. Then I took Atlantic Boulevard all the way to the drawbridge over the Intercoastal Waterway. The drawbridge was going up, and I sat at the red light watching the bridge rise up into the sky.

I got off my bike and walked it to the edge of the Intercoastal and watched this giant yacht approaching. The yacht had three 100-horsepower outboards and was rigged for deep-sea fishing and a fat guy in a white T-shirt was up on the bridge drinking Budweiser out of a can. I waved at him but he didn't wave back. On deck is a girl with long golden hair and golden eyes wearing a red bikini. She is knitting a blue wool sweater, and the yarn is dangling off the side of the yacht and into the water. She looks up at me and mouths the words *For you*. The yacht is drifting with the current and the fog is rolling in fast and I can't see the girl anymore. A foghorn blasts and I shout, *Sophie?* But she doesn't answer.

Then the drawbridge closed again. The lights stopped flashing and the barriers went back up and I rode my bike over the bridge back to the Mile. I went all the way past the cheesy tourist shops with signs that say SUNSCREEN BEANIE BABIES FRUITOPIA, and Niagara Towers where Pops lives, and finally came back to the ocean.

The stars were all out by then, and the wind was

rustling in the palms. I took off my shoes and walked right into the water and felt the foam surge around my ankles. Then I raised my arms up to the sky and shouted, "Hey, I'm alive!"

I know it sounds stupid, but that's what I did.

Out on Cocoabutter Creek I can hear a motorboat going past the house. Posie said she'd come by some night. I wonder if she'll come.

Sept. 7

I can't think of anything to write. I'm so tired of this.

I'm still a junior. What a loser.

Sept. 8, 2:37 A.M.

I'm writing this in the middle of the night when I should be sleeping. I went to bed around midnight, after the usual routine of food and homework and television. But then, at about 1 A.M., I heard someone knocking on the sliding glass door of my room.

"Hey, wake up. It's me."

I sat up, and saw Posie, standing outside with a big smile on her face. She was wearing a bikini top and cutoffs.

"Come on," she said. "Let's go for a ride."

"Posie?" I said, still kind of asleep. "It's the middle of the night."

"Best time for it," she said.

I pulled my pants on and went outside and followed her down the dock to her little motorboat. It isn't much of a boat, just an aluminum skiff with a 12-horsepower outboard that her father uses to get out to where their big sailboat is moored. The moon was nearly full, and it was warm, and the stars were amazing. I untied the bowline and jumped into the boat while Posie started up the outboard. Then we headed down Cocoabutter Creek.

"Hey, Posie," I said. "Where are we—"

"Hey, Jonah," she said. "Don't worry so much."

She handed me a thermos that was rolling around in the bottom of the boat. "Check this out," she said.

"What is it?" I asked. I didn't really feel like drinking.

"Try it."

I took a sip, expecting it to be whiskey or beer or something, but it wasn't. It was lemonade.

"Good, huh?"

It was more than good. I couldn't stop drinking it. It tasted like paradise.

"Homemade," Posie said. "From my Gammie's lemon trees. We picked the lemons this morning."

I imagined Posie waking up early to pick lemons with her grandma and cutting them in half and squeezing them into a big pitcher of ice water and adding the sugar and stirring it with a big wooden spoon in her sunny kitchen. I wished I could have been there.

We were in the Intercoastal now, passing underneath the drawbridge and out into the ocean. Waves lapped against the skiff, and the engine roared against the pull of the current.

A little ways out from shore was a strange glow on the surface of the water. At first I thought it was moonlight, but it wasn't. Posie steered the boat over to the patch of glowing water and cut the engine.

"I saw them tonight when I was surfing," Posie said. "I had a feeling they'd still be here."

"What?" I asked.

Posie pointed at the water.

"Jellies," she said.

I stared at the water, and it was full of huge, phosphorescent jellyfish. Their bodies were almost see-through, with luminous neon-green streaks. And they were glowing. It's really rare to see jellyfish in a big cluster like that because they can't really swim or control where they're going. They just float. I know jellyfish sound pretty disgusting, but seeing them out there in the quiet ocean with Posie in the moonlight, they were beautiful.

It was so cool that Posie knew how much I'd get off on seeing them, and that she would wake me up in the middle of the night so we could look at them. She's awesome.

I drank some more lemonade. Posie reached

down and ran her fingers over the surface of the water.

"They don't have stuff like this in Pennsylvania, do they, Jonah?" Posie said.

I told her no. They don't.

NORTHGIRL999: name / age / sex?

JBLACK94710: Jonah, 17, m

NORTHGIRL999: where are you?

JBLACK94710: Pompano beach, Florida. Where are you?

NORTHGIRL999: I am in Gnorsk.

JBLACK94710: Gnorsk?

NORTHGIRL999: Norway.

JBLACK94710: Norway? You're Norwegian?

NORTHGIRL999: yes.

JBLACK94710: say something in Norwegian.

NORTHGIRL999: Ar de dar demerna inte era systrar?

JBLACK94710: Ok. What's your name?

NORTHGIRL999: Aine.

JBLACK94710: Aine? How do I say that?

NORTHGIRL999: it rhymes with heiney. : D

JBLACK94710: how old are you?

NORTHGIRL999: 22. I am student at university of Stokholm.

JBLACK94710: what time is it there?

NORTHGIRL999: it is after four o'clock in the morning. What time in Florida?

JBLACK94710: 9:15 P.M. What are you doing up so late?

NORTHGIRL999: I can not to sleep. I had fight with this boyfriend.

JBLACK94710: I'm avoiding my German homework. I have a test tomorrow.

NORTHGIRL999: I took German in school. It is hard.

JBLACK94710: I don't think it's that hard. I'm in the accelerated section. I'm a senior.

JBLACK94710: so what do you do for fun in Norway?

NORTHGIRL999: I like music and books. And boys! I will send you my picture.

JBLACK94710: what music do you like?

NORTHGIRL999: have you heard of band called Smelts?

JBLACK94710: no way! They are my favorite band!

NORTHGIRL999: they perform here last month. I was in front row!

JBLACK94710: What's your favorite song?

NORTHGIRL999: I like Sheik of Araby.

JBLACK94710: Yes! Me too.

NORTHGIRL999: Did my picture get to there?

JBLACK94710: I'm downloading now. Wait, is that you?

NORTHGIRL999: That is me. :)

JBLACK94710: You are unbelievable.

NORTHGIRL999: I'm glad you like her!

JBLACK94710: nobody ever sent me a nude picture before.

NORTHGIRL999: so do you "cyber" Jonah Black? ;)

JBLACK94710: I don't know. What do we do?

NORTHGIRL999: you write out your fantasies. What comes to mind.

<u>JBLACK94710:</u> you want me to write my fantasies?

<u>NORTHGIRL999:</u> do you not have fantasies? I do.

<u>JBLACK94710:</u> Yes, but I don't really know you.

<u>NORTHGIRL999:</u> I feel like I know you, Jonah. I have been looking at your photograph for many months now. Diving board boy!

<u>JBLACK94710:</u> what are you talking about?

<u>NORTHGIRL999:</u> I am thinking about you ever since I saw your picture. I like your eyes.

<u>JBLACK94710:</u> You saw my picture?

<u>NORTHGIRL999:</u> You were in Masthead News on the Web. They have the photo of you on diving board. I love your photo Jonah!

<u>JBLACK94710:</u> Wow. I knew Masthead News was online, but I didn't know anyone read it.

<u>NORTHGIRL999:</u> I hope you do not think I am crazy Norwegian girl.

<u>JBLACK94710:</u> No, it's great. I was just surprised.

<u>NORTHGIRL999:</u> so play with me, Jonah. You have such sweet face. I think I have known you all my life.

<u>JBLACK94710:</u> You're very sweet, Aine.

<u>NORTHGIRL999:</u> so what would you do if we were together? Would you hold me?

<u>JBLACK94710:</u> yes, Aine. I would hold you close and kiss your cheek.

<u>NORTHGIRL999:</u> yes, Jonah, I can feel your soft lip on skin. I am running hands on back.

JBLACK94710: I can feel our bodies close together.

NORTHGIRL999: yes.

JBLACK94710: Now I'm looking deep into your eyes, amazed by their blue darkness.

NORTHGIRL999: oh Jonah. I am growing so drangk reading your words. Make love to me and let me be your Aine.

JBLACK94710: OK. Hang on a sec while I lock my door. I don't want my little sister coming in while we're doing this.

NORTHGIRL999: I will wait for you all night.

JBLACK94710: I'm back. So now I am again kissing your neck. And I am imagining that we are lying on a bed in front of a fire.

JBLACK94710: The flames are crackling and we are drinking wine with our bodies wrapped around each other.

JBLACK94710: we are in no rush because we know we have the whole night to make love over and over.

JBLACK94710: you put your hand on my chest and feel my heart beating and I look at you and I have never seen such beautiful eyes, ever.

JBLACK94710: are you still there?

JBLACK94710: hello?

JBLACK94710: Aine?

[NORTHGIRL999 is not currently signed on.]

Sept. 11

After writing practically a whole book in the first few days of school I've been avoiding this journal because it's too depressing. I'm still a junior and no one will listen to me. I asked Miss von Esse about it and all she said was if Mrs. Perella's made a "policy decision" there's nothing she can do about it. Mom and Honey don't even care, so I'm on my own. I'm beginning to get seriously worried because if I don't get put back in the senior class soon, it'll be too late. I've got to write to somebody in charge, like the principal, or the board of education.

Today was the first day of diving practice. The pool at Don Shula is actually pretty decent. A guy named Norton, from the Swimming Hall of Fame down in Ft. Lauderdale, donated all this money to build it and it's Olympic sized, with a three-meter board and a separate pool for the divers. Even Masthead didn't have that. This pool is so fancy they don't even call it the pool. They call it the natatorium, which is my new favorite word. Whenever I see Thorne I tell him I can't hang out, I have to do some serious time in the natatorium.

I think I'm going to like the men's swim coach, too, Mr. Davis. He actually got in the water and swam with us for a few laps. I've never seen a coach do that before. Usually the coach just stands there at the edge of the pool in a sweatshirt with a whistle and a clipboard, yelling at us. Mr. Davis told us for the first day he wanted us to just get in and have fun. Do laps, practice dives, whatever.

He said, "Remember, whatever else happens, sport is supposed to be fun. Jump in and mess around in the water, get yourselves reacclimated. There's going to be plenty of time this season for hard-core workouts. Today I want you to enjoy the pool and be glad you're here."

Then Mr. Davis whipped off his sweatshirt and his whistle and we all dove in and he dove in after us and we spent the whole practice just messing around. It was crazy. Of course, some of the guys did all these laps anyway, trying to break world records. But Mr. Davis didn't look all that impressed. After a couple of laps he got out and dried off and stood around watching us. Then he even went up to the high board and did two truly amazing dives. One of them was a double flip into a gainer. I guess it wasn't that big of a big deal, but it makes a huge difference knowing that our coach is at least as good a swimmer as the rest of us.

He also kept the divers and the lap swimmers together, which is a good idea. Usually coaches separate the divers from the swimmers like we're another team altogether and we do a whole different workout. But not Mr. Davis. This means that from the first day we're all working as a team, which is smart, I think.

Something else happened at practice. This girl I've never seen before, with straight black hair and really tan skin, a Native American maybe, was sitting in the bleachers. It sounds crazy, but I'm pretty sure she was watching me. I tried not to think about her, but every time I looked up, there she was, looking right at me with these big, dark eyes. I even made up an Indian name for her—Watches Boys Dive.

After practice I was going to go over and say hello, but she wasn't there anymore.

(Still Sept. 11, after school.)

When I got home from school, Mom was out, and there was a note from her on the table. *Read*

Chapter 11, the note said. *I love you, Jonah!* Next to the note was the copy of Mom's book.

I opened the book. Chapter eleven was titled "Self-Esteem Is Sexy."

"Jesus," I said out loud.

Honey came into the room. "Hey, Nutly. Looks like Mom is trying to give you a few pointers. It must be hard for her, talking to all those kids who are having sex like crazy, while her own son is like, a nun."

"Shut up," I said.

Honey got out a box of Ring Dings and stuffed one into her mouth. She was still wearing that dog collar thing around her neck.

"So are you all fine with Mom and this book?" I asked her.

"Sure. Why not?" Honey said.

"But aren't you like, embarrassed for her? What if she's exposed for being this sex-obsessed hippie freak who isn't even a Ph.D.?" I asked.

"Hey, she's got her own radio show," Honey said. "She's got a paperback deal. Sub rights. Ancillary products. Seems like she's doing pretty well for a freak."

"Ancillary products? What the hell are ancillary products?" I said.

"You know, like shampoo and popcorn with her

name on the label," Honey explained. "Maybe Kmart'll come out with a Dr. Judith line of teen sex toys. They might even make her a spokesperson for Wendy's. I'd drink a Frosty out of a cup with Mom's face on it. Wouldn't you?"

She went to the refrigerator and got out a gallon bottle of Jolt cola, unscrewed the top, and guzzled it, her pale throat rippling. Then she wiped her mouth, screwed the cap back on, and put the Jolt back in the refrigerator.

"So you think it's fine that she's pretending to be some big sex expert?" I asked.

"I think that's called a sexpert," Honey said.

"Whatever."

"I don't care what she does," Honey explained. "I'm out of here in ten months. Once I'm in college, she can call herself a plumber for all I care."

"But this is worse than pretending to be a plumber," I said. "She could get in trouble."

"Oh, what's the big deal?" said Honey. "What do you care? Let Mom have a career. It's better than her sitting around the house doing yoga. You should have seen what it was like before she did this book. All these tripped-out divorced women sitting around the living room chanting "Ommmmm."

"But what does Mom know about teen sex?" I asked.

Honey reached into her pocket and pulled out a hard pack of Camel Lights. She stuck one in her mouth, and lit it with a lighter.

"She doesn't have to know anything," said Honey. "Not much, anyway."

"But what if she's giving people like, bad information? She might be telling them the wrong things."

Honey smiled. "Don't worry, I checked the pages before the book went to press. I fixed all the mistakes."

It didn't sound like Honey was talking about spelling mistakes.

"You rewrote *Hello Penis! Hello Vagina!*?"

"Just the parts that were totally ignorant."

"Does Mom know?" I couldn't believe it. I guess Honey's the one who should have her own talk show.

She shrugged. "Beats me."

I just stared at her for a moment.

"Hey, Honey. Since when do you smoke?" I asked.

"I don't," she said, blowing a smoke ring at me.

"You know Mom is going to freak when she comes home and smells cigarettes. She's going to give you a big lecture on how you're not valuing your personhood or whatever."

"Not me," Honey said. "You're the one smoking."

"Me?"

"Yeah, you. I'm in the genius section. She isn't going to think I'm dumb enough to be smoking Camels right in the kitchen."

"You're really evil, you know that?" I said.

"Yeah," said Honey. "But you love me anyway."

Now I'm thinking of actually reading Mom's book. Oh, my God, I can't believe I even wrote that. Forget it.

I'm in Miss von Esse's class and she's going through the list of modal auxiliaries in German— can, must, like to, allowed to, should, would. This is one of the few things I definitely know how to do in this stupid language. Sometimes I wish I'd taken something other than German, I mean especially at Don Shula, where you can take Portuguese or Japanese if you want to. I mean, why German?

Well, I know why. I took German here freshman year, and at the time I was pretty good at it. Then at Masthead the only alternatives were French or Latin, and I've never been very good at them. It kind of figures I'm no good at Romance languages. Anyway, my German teacher there was this real hardass. Plus, Sophie O'Brien was in the class with me, so it was kind of hard to concentrate.

Thorne said something kind of weird to me this morning. He was walking to homeroom with Luna Hayes and he saw me and came over, while Luna went on to the Zoo.

"Hey, Luna's been asking about you," Thorne said.

"Yeah?" I said. "How come?"

"She wants to know if you'd ever want to visit the firehouse with her."

"The firehouse?"

"Yeah. She's totally into it. You let me know, I can get you guys in there, okay?" Thorne said, his face totally serious.

I just kind of laughed and Thorne said, "Later," and walked off.

I still don't know if he was serious or not, but it definitely sounded like he was.

See, the whole time I was at Masthead, Thorne and I wrote all these stupid e-mails about our sexual encounters. Like I'd write about being in an apple orchard doing it on the ground with this farm girl and every time she made a sound like *ooh*, another apple would fall to the ground. And then Thorne would write about doing it with the girl who feeds the seals at the Miami Zoo and when she orgasmed the seals all went up on their hind legs and started slapping their flippers together and barking. The e-mails kept getting wilder and dumber and dirtier. And they were all a bunch of lies. At least I thought they were.

But one of the e-mails Thorne sent me was about Luna Hayes and how she liked to have sex on the fire trucks at the Pompano Beach Fire Station. Thorne said the chief of police owed his dad a favor because of something he'd been caught doing at Thorne's dad's motel, so whenever Thorne wanted he could go into the volunteer fire station after hours and do it with Luna.

I had always thought this was another big lie. I mean, Thorne's stories were so dumb and farfetched it never occurred to me to take them seriously. And Luna was always this skinny little kid, not the babe he described, so it seemed totally bogus. But guess what? I think I'm wrong about all of it. Luna really *does* like to do it in the fire station. And Thorne really did have sex with all those girls in all those crazy places while I didn't do anything. I was lying my ass off the whole time.

So I wonder if Thorne believed what I was writing. Does he think I'm like, this big stud?

Sept. 13

Mom and I had a little talk after school today. She came into my room while I was doing homework, and said, "Jonah, honey, we need to talk."

"Okay," I said.

"I know you want people to accept you," she said. "It's an important thing for a boy. Especially one with your . . . issues."

"Mom!" I was worried she was going to bring up the underwear thing.

"Bup, bup," she said, holding out her hand. "But you must follow the rules of this house, and respect them. Respecting the rules of the house means you're respecting yourself. You do want to respect yourself, don't you?"

I sighed. It was easier not to argue. "I do," I said.

"All right then. There is to be no more smoking in this house. Do you understand?"

"Smoking?" I said. "Mom, I'm not—"

"Bup, bup, bup," she said. "Let's not play the Honesty Game. Okay? I won't have it."

"All right," I said. "We won't play the Honesty Game."

"When you smoke, you are saying that your body is a manure pile. A trash heap. And I won't have you disrespecting yourself. Do you understand?"

"Yes, Mom," I said. "I understand."

She took a deep breath, held it, and exhaled. Then she came over and hugged me. "You're a special person, Jonah," she said.

Honey came to the door. "What's happening?" she asked.

"Nothing, Pumpkin," Mom said. "Jonah and I were talking. Weren't we?"

"We were," I said.

"I need for Jonah to know his body isn't a garbage dump. Will you help him, Honey? Make sure he doesn't smoke in the house and.send out a signal to everyone that he's not valuable?"

"I'll help him with his signals," Honey said.

"That's my angel," said Mom.

She hugged us both, one with each arm. "I have two special kids," she said.

"You know it," Honey said.

Dr. Aristotle Chamberlin
Principal, Don Shula High School
Pompano Beach, FL 33092
September 13

Dear Dr. Chamberlin,

Recently I was informed that I was to be a junior at Don Shula this year instead of a senior. I believe an injustice has been committed. I want to petition you to reconsider this decision because it is unfair and detrimental to my education.

It was explained to me by Mrs. Perella that I did not finish up my junior year at Masthead Academy in "good standing" and therefore I cannot get credit. However, I took all of my final exams there except for German, so I should get credit for the year.

Mrs. Perella said that because Don Shula is a magnet school in languages, my German grade was the one that really made a difference. Although I did get a D for the year I would have gotten a higher grade if I had been able to take the final exam for that course. But I had to leave the day of the exam, which wasn't my fault.

I believe I have performed adequately as a student and should be a senior because, no matter how the year ended for me, I am a good student and do not deserve to be in the eleventh grade again. I want to go to college next year.

I hope you will consider my request to be moved back up to the senior class. I'd be grateful to talk to you about this at your earliest convenience, or sooner.

Sincerely,

Jonah Black

I almost didn't mail this to Dr. Chamberlin because I was afraid it sounded desperate. But then I realized I am desperate. I'm doing the Civil War for the second time in American history and I can't stand it.

So I mailed it. Of course it's still possible that Dr. Chamberlin might not even exist, since no one's ever seen him. If that's true, then this letter is completely worthless.

Sept. 14

After school I walked down to the beach to watch
Posie surf with her team. It was a whole big scene
down there. People were hanging out, lying on towels,
listening to music, drinking beer on the sly, smoking.
Not everybody was from Don Shula, but I recognized
some of them. There were people from Pompano
Latin and Ely High and Milhaus Community College.
A lot of the kids who usually hang out in the IHOP.

So Thorne and I stood on the beach watching
Posie and Wailer and Lindsey LeFarge, this other
girl from Don Shula. Posie is so damn good. I
mean, when she dropped down into the shoulder of
a wave everybody on the beach got quiet and
watched her, and when she finished up, people
applauded. To be honest, there was some of the

same admiration for Wailer, but when he surfed everybody just nodded and cheered. Posie made people fall silent.

"She's the golden girl," Thorne said.

"I know," I said.

"Hey," Thorne said, perking up. "You don't have the hots for Posie, do you?"

"Thorne," I said, like it was the stupidest thing he'd ever asked me. "Get real. She's my friend."

"Well, I'm trying to get you back into form," Thorne said. "I bet Posie would do it with you if you asked her."

"Hey," I said, really annoyed now. "She's in love with Wailer, okay?"

"Yeah. You're right," Thorne said. "She probably wouldn't do it with you after all."

"Well, what'd you bring it up for then?" I snapped.

"I don't know, Jonah," Thorne said. "I yam vast. I contain multitudes."

"Are you high or something?" I had no idea what he was talking about.

"Dude," Thorne said. "It's Walt Whitman. The poet? Oh," he said, pretending to be embarrassed. "I forgot they don't teach Whitman in eleventh grade!"

"You're enjoying this, aren't you?" I said, glaring at him. "You think it's funny that I'm a junior."

"You want to know the truth?" Thorne said. "I think it bites worse than you do. I was looking forward to having you around, Jonah. Classes suck."

We both watched as Posie glided across the water on her surfboard. Talk about poetry.

"How'd you like to be able to do something that well?" I said.

Thorne smiled wickedly. "Dude, I already do."

"What?" I said. But now that I think about it I know what he was talking about.

Right about then, Lucy McIntyre walked over to us.

"Hi, Thorne," she said. "You going to Luna's Friday?"

Thorne frowned, like he was really stressed about his superbusy schedule. "I don't know," he said. "I got a lot going on." He is so full of it sometimes.

"Okay," Lucy said, flustered. "Call me, okay?"

"I'll try," Thorne said.

"Maybe I could come over to your house before the party. And then we could go over together," she suggested.

Thorne frowned again, but this time it looked real.

"Friday's not a good day," he said. "At least not to come over."

"Thorne," Lucy said, and now her voice sounded desperate. "Call me?"

"Okay," Thorne said. "Whatever."

Lucy walked away, her shoulders slumped. I felt sorry for her.

"Hey, Thorne," I said. "What was that about?"

"Just keeping her guessing," Thorne said, like it was no big deal.

"But I thought you liked her. I thought you were going out with her."

"I am," he said. "Come on, Jonah, don't tell me you don't ever give the tuna a little yank on the line?"

"Tuna?" I said.

He nodded, like it was the one thing he knew for sure in the universe. "Tuna," he said.

"But you are going to Luna's, right?"

"Absolutely, are you kidding? Her parents are going to France. It's the first certified blowout of the fall season."

"So why didn't you tell Lucy you were going?"

But Thorne wasn't listening anymore. He was looking at this tall girl wearing a St. Winnifred's Academy uniform, standing on the beach a few feet away.

"Uh-oh. I gotta go," Thorne said. Then he got up and walked over to talk to the girl. Something about Thorne seemed weird to me. I feel like I'm not getting the whole story from him sometimes. But then again, I haven't exactly given him my whole story either, so I guess we're even.

I stood around for a little while longer and then I got my bike and walked it along the shore toward Lighthouse Point. Seeing Posie surfing made me feel kind of depressed. It's like I'm jealous of her, not for being such a good surfer, but for knowing exactly what she wants to do. I mean I wouldn't be surprised if she did wind up dropping out and going pro and living with Wailer on the beach and making babies. Maybe that's what she's meant to do.

I guess it makes me sad that our lives have gone in such different directions, too. Three years ago, Posie and Thorne and I were pretty much inseparable. And now Thorne is this smooth operator and Posie is a surfer goddess and I'm this loser who looks exactly the same as he did in ninth grade.

There's really nothing wrong with our lives going in different directions. I just wish mine was going forward instead of backward.

I reached the old lifeguard tower and leaned my bike against the base and climbed up the ladder. There was a big brown pelican perched on the lifeguard bench, but it took off when it saw me.

A moment later I heard someone singing, " 'Hello young lovers, wherever you are. . . . I've had a love like yours. . . .' "

Then a Red Sox cap came bobbing up the ladder. It was Pops Berman.

"Move over," he said, and I shoved over on the bench so the old man could sit down.

"Hi, Pops," I said.

"Hello, Chipper." Pops wheezed throatily. He looked tired.

"How's it going?" I asked.

"Lousy," he said.

"Lousy? How come?"

"What? You want a list? Kidneys, failing. Liver, failing. Gall bladder—hell, kid, I haven't seen my gall bladder in forty years! I'm a mess!" He started coughing into his fist.

I felt bad for him. "I'm sorry, Pops. Have you seen a doctor?" I asked.

"A doctor? Ha! You know what they tell me? Lay off the booze! Lay off the coffee! Lay off the cigars! Lay off the doughnuts! What? Are they trying to kill me?"

"Well, what you eat does kind of affect your health," I said.

"What am I gonna do with health? Tell me that? I'm supposed to eat twigs and berries so I can keep on doing *this*?" He coughed into his fist again. Then he whacked me with this wooden cane he carries around but doesn't really use. "It's you I'm worried about, kid. You're in a state, aren't you, Chipper? You're pathetic."

"What are you talking about?" I said, rubbing my arm where he'd hit me.

"I seen you down at the surfing beach standing all by yourself, watching that girl with the pumpkin butt out on the waves. You're not going to let her walk your doggy, are you? You're too darn stupid."

"Posie? You're talking about Posie?" I said, a little freaked out that he'd been watching me.

"I don't know what her name is. All I know is, you've given up. You aren't even trying! Goddammit, I don't understand you. Look at you, you got all the catnip in the world! Young fella, good-looking, not too stupid. And you're just letting her get away. You think you're going to be proud of yourself when you're like me? A disgusting old derelict? Well?"

The conversation was getting ridiculous. "She has a boyfriend, Pops," I said.

"Oh, I don't give a goddamn about her boyfriend. Don't talk to me about her boyfriend! Don't . . ." He stood up, heading for the ladder.

"Where are you going?" I said.

"I gotta get away from you, Chipper. You're making me too mad. I'm gonna get a heart attack and drop dead this instant if I don't stop talking to you."

"I thought you didn't care about dying," I said.

"I don't care if I die, I just don't want to do it today."

But I didn't want him to leave. I wanted to hear what he had to say. "Wait. Stop," I said. "You think I should go after Posie?"

Pops leaned against the railing and adjusted his baseball cap. "Tell me the thought's never entered your mind," he said.

I sat there for a while, not sure what to say. The old guy is definitely sharp. He's practically psychic.

"Okay," I said. "So I've thought about it."

"Atta boy. Now you get in there and start walkin' the doggy!" Pops shouted.

"I don't know, Pops. It's different with Posie. She's my friend," I said. "I've known her since we were eight."

"Exactly!" said Pops. "Who else are you gonna play hide-the-salami with? Some girl you don't even know?"

"She's taken," I said. "She's in love. She wants to live on the beach with her boyfriend and make babies."

Pops just shook his head. "I don't know what's more pathetic. That she believes him, or that you believe her."

"You think he's lying?" I said.

Pops just laughed. "Hmm. Let me think. Yeah,

it's a big mystery, all right. That's his *line*, stupid. I bet he's used it a thousand times."

This was the best news I'd heard in a long time, but also the worst. I didn't like to think that Posie was being played.

Pops coughed into his fist again. "Let me ask you one question, Chipper. What did I tell you last time? About why we're here, the purpose of life?"

I remembered what he'd said. "To love women?" I said.

Pops nodded, and his face took on a happy glow. "You've got it. What the hell. Maybe you aren't so stupid as I thought."

"All women?" I said.

Pops smiled even wider. "Oh, yes," he said, with an expression of bliss and utter calm. "All women."

He climbed down the ladder and as he walked away I heard him singing again.

Now I'm back home again and I'm writing this in my room and I have this crazy feeling that Pops Berman might be right about Posie. But as soon as I start thinking about being with her I feel like I'm entering forbidden territory and I kind of stop myself. Maybe I should be on some of those drugs Cheese Girl was talking about. I need to relax.

Sept. 15

I went to work at First Amendment today and I knew something was up because Mr. Swede wasn't there and Mrs. Swede kept referring to him as "zat *man*." I wonder if they're getting divorced. I always thought they were perfectly happy together, but who knows. I guess you can never tell with couples. I don't remember Mom and Dad ever fighting. It was like they were together and then suddenly Dad wasn't coming home anymore. Then one Sunday Mom sat us down and told us Dad was moving to Pennsylvania. I kept waiting for her to tell us when he was coming back, but she didn't.

I had five pizzas to deliver—two pepperoni, one regular, a sausage, and one veggie. The pepperonis went to a small brick house in Cresthaven. A girl answered the door wearing a long Japanese robe.

Her house was full of little yellow birds singing in cages.

She had me wait in the hall while she got the money. I could smell incense burning and I could hear water trickling in a fountain but I couldn't see it. The girl came back carrying a tray with a tea service on it and she says, "Would you like some tea?" and I nod my head yes. I take my shoes off and follow her into a garden with a flagstone floor and little wind chimes hanging in the trees. The girl kneels down to pour the tea into tiny cups without handles. Her hair is pulled tight into a ponytail and there are tiny diamond studs in her ears.

A white horse nibbles at a flowering bush in the garden. It stamps its foot and snorts.

Sophie holds out a cup and I take it and the tea is warm and tastes like licorice.

"There's more," Sophie says. "Do you want some more?"

"Yes," I say. "Please."

As she leans over to pour the tea her robe falls open and I take the kettle out of her hand and put it on the floor. Sophie kneels in front of me and says, "Jonah Black opening the door of love to enter the green ocean of bliss and homecoming." Then she begins to unbutton my shirt. Japanese music tinkles in the background, and I close my eyes.

"I'm sorry, the birds are so noisy tonight, I didn't hear you. Would you like some tea?" the girl asked, tucking her thick brown hair behind her ears.

"No, thank you," I told her. "I have more pizzas to deliver."

I got back on my bike and rode down Dixie to an apartment in a four-story building across from the airport. It was full of all these college girls smoking a big bong in their underwear, and they were laughing their heads off. The girl that paid me was giggling so hard she had to put the sausage and the regular on the floor and sit down to try to get control of herself. Her friends were all howling at her like it was the funniest thing they had ever seen. I didn't say anything. It was none of my business.

The last delivery was at a nice-looking stucco house near Kester Park. At first I didn't think anybody was home. I had to ring the bell like three or four times and this little dog was barking like crazy. Finally a girl shouted from an upstairs window, "I'll be right down, come on in." A cloud of steam drifted out the window as she called to me, and her hair was wet.

So I went in and stood in the front hallway, waiting for her but she didn't come down. I could hear the water running and I kept waiting for it to shut off and for her to come down the stairs, but nothing happened. This little brown toy poodle kept running around my legs going *"Gwipe gwipe gwipe."* Finally, I walked over to the bottom of the stairs and yelled, "Hello?" I heard this kind of frustrated sigh of exasperation. So I shouted, "Are you okay?"

"Would you mind coming up here for a second?" the girl called back.

So I climbed the stairs. It was a very nice house, with green wall-to-wall carpeting and white walls, and it looked like no one else was home. The little dog followed me and when I got to the top I said, "Hello?"

The girl came out of the bathroom with her hair in a towel, wearing a white terry cloth bathrobe.

"Are you all right?" I said.

"I'm okay, it's nothing, forget it," she said. "How much do I owe you?"

"Thirteen dollars," I said.

She dug around in her wallet and handed me fifteen bucks.

"Thanks," I said, and turned to go.

Then she says, "Can I ask you a question?"

"Sure," I say.

"Do you think you could put some of this lotion on my back?" she asks. "There's this one spot right in the middle and no matter what I do I can't reach it."

She hands me a bottle of Lubriderm and I squirt

some on my hand. Then she turns her back and lets her robe drop to her hips. I run my hand over her pale, freckled shoulders. Her skin is very soft but I can feel the hardness of her bones underneath. I cover her back with lotion and then she turns around.

"Do my front, too," she says.

So I squirt more lotion into my hands and rub her chest and her stomach, trying to be professional about it.

And then she says, "Now I'm going to do you, Jonah Black." So I take off my shirt and she starts rubbing the lotion on me but it's disappearing fluid, and everywhere she spreads it, I disappear. She works all the way down my body until I'm just a pair of shins and feet, and then she does those and I'm totally gone. Then she fills her hands with the thick cream and rubs it all over her face and arms and stomach and legs, until she disappears, too. I feel an invisible kiss, a kiss without any bodies at all. And Sophie whispers, *You see, this is the only way we can be together, if we're totally invisible.*

Sept. 18

I'm sitting in Miss von Esse's homeroom, waiting for the day to begin. I've been an eleventh grader almost two weeks now. I haven't heard anything from Dr. Chamberlin. You'd think if someone didn't exist they'd at least have the courtesy to let you know.

Last night I overheard Mom on the phone with someone and it sounded kind of suspicious. At first I thought it might be her agent, or someone down at the radio station, but then I realized that she was doing something I'd never heard her do before. Mom, the famous author, the famous Dr. Judith, was *flirting*.

"Oh, stop," she said, giggling like a twelve-year-old. "*Stop* it. You're terrible!"

Then there was silence for a little bit, followed

by more insane giggling. I was sitting in the kitchen, eating a Twinkie, trying to read the comics. While I was sitting there, Honey walked in.

"Are you listening to this?" she said, sitting down across from me. She opened a can of Jolt cola and got a package of Skittles out of her backpack.

"To what?" I said, without looking up.

"This crap," Honey said. She tilted her head back and poured the entire package of Skittles into her mouth. She chewed it for a while like gum.

"I don't know what you're talking about," I said.

In the next room, Mom was talking in a baby voice. She sounded like Tweetie Bird. "I really, really am?" she said. "Oh, you silly. Of course you're my favorite."

"Our mother thinks she's Malibu Barbie," Honey said. She stuck out her tongue. It was purple.

"Ooh," Mom said. "You are so bad!"

"You think this is covered in *Hello Penis*?" Honey said. She pulled a copy of Mom's book off the shelf and checked the index. "What should I look under? Maybe *M* for 'Middle-aged Horny Housewives'?" She shook her head. "No listing. Oh, yeah, I forgot, this book is about teenagers, Mom's specialty."

"Stop it!" Mom said, laughing hysterically. "I'm serious! You're going to make me wet my pants."

"That's it," Honey said, standing up. "I'm outta here." She grabbed her keys.

"Take me with you!" I said, jumping to my feet.

"Sorry, Squidly," Honey said. "You're not invited."

"Where?" I demanded.

Honey smiled. "Football practice."

She headed out, and a second later I saw the Jeep whiz by the kitchen widow. I have got to get my license back.

Mom hung up the phone and came into the kitchen. "Hi, Jonah," she said. "How are you?"

"I'm all right," I said.

"No, how are you *really*?" Mom said, looking concerned.

"I'm still all right," I insisted.

She picked up the copy of *Hello Penis! Hello Vagina!* that Honey had left lying on the table and turned it over to look at her author photo on the back. She was wearing a yellow suit in the photo. Her hair had been highlighted, and her makeup was professionally done. She looked kind of like Martha Stewart, with an insane gleam in her eye.

"Jonah, be honest. Do you think I look fat in this picture?"

"No, Mom, you look great," I said. "Who was that on the phone?"

"On the phone?" Mom said, all innocent.

"Yes," I said. "The person you were just talking to."

"Just a friend," she said, and blushed. That's when I knew something was up, because nothing makes Mom blush. I mean she tells people on her radio show how to masturbate. And here she was, turning red because I asked her who she was talking to on the *telephone*?

"What kind of friend?" I said.

"Jonah," Mom said. "It's not nice to eavesdrop."

"I wasn't eavesdr—"

"Bup, bup, bup," she said, holding out her hand.

"Okay," I said. "Sorry."

"Jonah," Mom said, sitting down across from me. "This is a hard time to be a boy, isn't it?"

"A hard time?" I repeated.

"Yes." She looked at me with big sympathetic eyes. "You know I'm always here for you, don't you? I'm always ready to listen?"

"Yes, Mom," I said.

"Because after what happened at your boarding school, I worry about you," she said.

"I'm all right," I said. I hesitated. And for a split second I actually considered confiding in her, just telling her everything that was on my mind.

Then her cell phone rang again.

"Hello?" she said. Then her voice went up like five octaves. "Oh hiiiiiiii, agaaaaaain. You're not supposed to have this number!"

Mom put her hand over the receiver.

"I have to take this," she said, and went back to her room.

I have to stop writing. Miss von Esse has called me to the board to conjugate the verb "to listen" in German. She's a pretty sharp teacher.

Sept. 19

We had another preseason practice today. Watches Boys Dive was there again, and she was wearing a suede shirt that looked so soft it was almost liquid. Again I was sure she was watching me. And again she disappeared before I got a chance to talk to her. I asked Martino Suarez about her after practice, but he said he hadn't noticed anyone. Now I'm thinking she's like my Indian spirit guide or something, which sounds like a nice idea. It would be nicer, though, if she was real.

I started showing off for Watches Boys Dive today, and pulled off this wicked hard dive—a back two-and-a-half somersault with a one-and-a-half twist. It's a Division I dive, the best one I know. I'd only done it right like four times at Masthead, and I hadn't tried it once since I came back to Florida. But today I did it perfectly. Mr. Davis was definitely impressed.

"You pulled that one out of the hat, Mr. Black," he said. "You're full of surprises, aren't you?"

I just smiled like it was no big deal.

Then Mr. Davis pulled me aside. "Jonah, that's a dangerous dive to do unless you're ready," he said. "I don't want you pulling any stunts until you're in shape. That means physically and mentally, all right?"

"Okay," I agreed.

"The last thing we need is for you to knock your head on the board, so we have to haul you off to the hospital. You know where that will leave us?"

I nodded. I knew where it would leave us: nowhere. I'm kind of the strongest diver on the team right now.

Later on, I saw Thorne in the weight room, which was weird because I've never seen him work out. It was just me and Martino, and a couple of other guys from the swim team doing our reps. Suddenly Thorne strolls in with his Discman on so loud I could hear the music. He lay down on the bench press and started lifting. He could barely lift 120.

"Hey, Thorne," I said. "What are you doing?"

He smiled. "Ah, nothing, just working up a little sweat. Got a big night with Elanor Brubaker. She likes it when my hair's a little sweaty."

"You're in here because you're trying to make your hair sweaty?" I said, laughing.

"You got a better method?"

"You could just wet your hair with water. What's the difference?" I said.

Thorne shook his head like I was hopelessly clueless. "Whatever," he said.

I watched him struggle with the bench press, and tried to spot him a little.

Thorne did about six repetitions and then let the barbell drop with a clang. He sat up and took a drink from his water bottle. "Hey, Jonah," he said. "You ever talk to that girl you were so into up at Masthead?"

"Who? Sophie?" I said.

"Yeah, that's her. Sophie," Thorne said.

I was glad I was still kind of wet from diving, because I suddenly broke out into this horrible, cold sweat.

"Nah. I tried to call her at home a few times but there was no answer," I said. "And her e-mail doesn't work either. Maybe they moved or something." It was all lies. I hadn't been in touch with Sophie because I had no idea what to say to her.

"Why don't you just call her at school?" Thorne said. "They have phones in Pennsylvania, right?"

"I don't want anyone there to know," I stammered. "It's complicated."

"I could find her home number for you," Thorne offered. "I love doing stuff like that."

My heart was doing the butterfly in my stomach. I was suddenly very cold.

"Sure," I said. "Whatever."

"Okay," Thorne said. "Sophie what? What's her last name?"

"O'Brien," I told him.

"And where is she from? What state?"

"Maine," I said quietly.

"O'Brien, in Maine," Thorne said. "I can probably find her. But if I do, you're going to explain this whole big mystery to me, right?"

"Maybe," I said. "Just find the number."

Suddenly I couldn't wait. If I had Sophie's home telephone number I could call her over Fall break maybe, and explain everything to her. We could arrange to meet. Things could still work out.

"All right," Thorne said. "I'll get my men working on it."

"Since when do you have men, Thorne?" I laughed.

"Dude, I got stuff you wouldn't believe," he said, laughing, too. His beeper went off and he pulled it out of his pocket. "Whoa, dude, it's Elanor. Gotta go. I'll talk to you later."

As I continued my reps, I kept hearing the words *O'Brien, in Maine*, over and over.

---■---

Sept. 20

I'm lying in bed writing by the light of my crappy bedside lamp. It's after one in the morning. Posie was just here. The whole room still smells like her—like saltwater and sunscreen.

I was finishing my German homework when I heard a boat out on the canal and a light drawing up to the dock and two seconds later there she is, knocking on the glass. I love the way she just shows up.

Her hair was wet and she had this big grin on her face. "Can I come in?" she said.

I slid open the door and she came in. She was wearing the top half of a red string bikini and that purple sarong skirt I'd seen her wear before and no shoes. I stopped for a second, just taking her in.

"Jeez, Jonah, stop staring at my boobs," she

said, but she didn't sound mad. She just stood there watching me drink her up.

"I hope you don't mind me coming over," she said. "I was out night-surfing. It was so completely gnarly, I couldn't see a thing. How are you doing, anyway?"

"I'm all right," I said.

"Hey, do you mind if I sit down on your bed? I'm still a little wet from surfing."

I moved my books out of the way, and she sat down and leaned her back against the wall. She looked around my room.

"I've missed having you around, Jonah. You're the only person in the universe I can talk to," she said.

"What about Thorne? He didn't go anywhere," I said.

"Oh, well, Thorne is a sweetheart, but you know what he's like. All he wants to do is talk about sex all the time. It kind of wears me down after a while, to tell you the truth."

I liked that Posie said that. I wanted to be the one she talked to. But what about Wailer? What was she going out with him for if she couldn't talk to him? I didn't say anything, though. I didn't want to piss her off, and I really didn't want her to leave. She might be my best friend, but I couldn't help staring at the way the salt had crusted on her eyelashes, like crystals. In the hollows of her collarbone, too. She looked like a mermaid.

"You want a chaw?" Posie asked, and I snapped out of it. I don't think she caught me looking. Or if she did, she didn't mind.

"No, thanks. But you go ahead," I said.

She filled her cheek with chewing tobacco, then reached down her bikini top and scratched under her breasts. It seems like she is always scratching them in front of me. I guess it's nice that Posie feels comfortable around me.

"This top is murder. You don't have a T-shirt I could borrow, do you?" she asked.

I walked over to my dresser and got a plain white T-shirt from the second drawer and tossed it to her. Posie stood up, turned her back to me, and picked at the back of her bikini.

"Damn. Can you untie this thing for me?"

"Sure." I worked at the knot, which was hard to undo because it was wet, and my hands were sort of trembling. When it came loose Posie let the top fall onto the floor and for just a second I saw her bare back. I think a girl's bare back has got to be the most incredible thing in the world. I mean, part of it is just the drama of knowing how cool it would be if they turned around. But their backs also look so delicate and vulnerable you just want to touch them. Posie's does, anyway.

Posie pulled my shirt over her head and turned around and sat back down on the bed. My shirt definitely looked better on her than on me.

"That's better," she said. One of her cheeks was full of tobacco. She looked like Popeye the Sailor Man. "So what's the story with the girl in Pennsylvania? Are you two still seeing each other?"

"Sophie," I said. "You mean Sophie?"

"Yeah. What's up with her?" Posie said.

I felt my ears getting hot. I didn't know what to tell her.

Posie looked at me and poked me in the arm. "Jonah. You're shaking," she said.

"Um, I d-don't know what to say," I stuttered. "We kind of had a misunderstanding."

Posie stood up and spat a big squirt of juice out the window into my mother's shrubs. Then she sat down next to me on the bed.

"Jonah, babe, it sounds like you really loved her," she said.

"I think I did, Posie," I said. "I think I'm a little messed up now."

My voice choked a little, and Posie gave me this great big hug. It felt great, the best feeling I've had since I came back.

"You know what you need, Jonah? You need . . . excuse me." She went to the window again and spat out another big squirt of juice. "You need a woman."

"Yeah, well, Thorne has me all lined up with his ex-girlfriends," I said.

"That's not what I mean. I mean somebody of your own," Posie said. She looked at her watch. "Oh, my God, it's almost one in the morning. I've got to go."

She slid open the glass door and blew the rest of the tobacco juice out into my mother's hydrangeas. "Don't worry, Jonah. We'll work it out," she said, turning back to me. Then she came back over to the bed and gave me another big hug and kissed me on the lips.

"You'd better not have a boner, or I'm going to punch your lights out," she said.

"I'm fine. Believe me. I hardly even notice you're a girl," I said. It's funny. I didn't used to notice Posie was a girl, but I do now. It's painful.

"I'm a girl?" Posie said, in shock, and looked down at her chest. "Oh, my God! You're right!"

Then she ran outside, and a second later I heard her boat roar on up the creek.

I looked at the place where she'd been sitting on the bed. There were two wet butt cheek marks on my sheets.

Then I looked down at the floor. She'd left her bikini top behind.

My bedroom door creaked open and my sister poked her head into the room.

"Can I come in here, Lamo, or are you jerking off?" Honey said.

"Come on in," I said.

Honey opened the door. She was wearing a black T-shirt with a skull on it that said HARLEY-DAVIDSON.

"So. Who's your friend?" she asked me.

"I don't know what you're talking about," I said, trying to be mysterious.

"You're telling me some girl didn't just spit tobacco juice out your window?"

"A girl? No," I said.

Honey walked into the room and picked Posie's bikini top up off the floor. She held it up.

"This is really cute," she said. "You'll definitely look hot in this."

"It's Posie's," I said, bored with our little game. "She stopped in on her way back from surfing."

"She's loaning you her stuff now?" Honey said. "Man, that's open-minded."

She examined Posie's bikini top carefully and whistled.

"Up yours," I said.

"Hey, you want to borrow any of my undies? You want to start wearing girls' panties to school every day, you just say the word."

"Did you want something, or did you just come in here to annoy me?" I said.

"Listen, Phlegmball, can I ask you a question?" Honey said.

"Anything for you," I said.

"What's that chick like, that Dad married?" Honey said.

I was surprised. Honey always acts so tough. After Dad moved out, she pretty much pretended she forgot about him.

"Tiffany? I don't know. She's young, I guess. You'd say she's young," I said.

"Like what? Six, seven years old?" Honey said.

"I think she's twenty-three."

"His secretary," she said.

"His former secretary," I corrected her. I was watching Honey's face to see how this information was affecting her, but she seemed unmoved.

"And so what, he like, buys her horses, jewelry, that kind of thing?" she said.

"Yeah. Well, they're married and all."

Honey stood there looking at her nails. Some of them were pretty long. She had this kind of blank expression.

"You think he's gonna call me on my birthday?" she asked me.

"Sure, he will," I said, although I wasn't at all sure. Dad's not exactly the most thoughtful person in the world.

"Well, he can call or he can not call. I don't give a crap," Honey said.

"You could call *him*," I said.

"Yeah. Right. Hey listen, is there anything I can do for you, Spazmo? Is there anything you want? Cuban cigars? The answers to the SAT? What?"

I noticed she was changing the subject, but that was all right. There was something I wanted. Badly.

"I want to be a senior," I told her.

"A senior? You mean like, you need me to break into the master record room, forge a bunch of documents from Masthead, alter your transcript, that kind of thing?"

"Yeah," I said hopefully. "Could you do that? I mean, seriously? Could you?"

"You mean like I could get my hacker friends to crack the school's computer, and make the changes?" she said.

"Yes," I said, getting excited. "Can you do that? Please?"

She shrugged. "Sorry, Nutly. I can't hack into the school's computer."

"How do you know if you haven't tried?"

Honey smiled. "You think I haven't tried?"

She went to the door. "If you change your mind about the panties thing, though, let me know."

Then she walked back to her room, and I crawled into bed and wrote this. Now I'm going to sleep.

Sept. 21

Today was my second session at Amerishrinks. That same girl was waiting in the lobby today, but this time she didn't look up at me and when her mother came out of her session the girl didn't even wait for her, she just got up and headed toward the car. I wondered what the two of them would talk about in the car ride home. I bet they're going through some big conflict right now and the mother is seeing Dr. LaRue to help her with it, although she really wants her daughter to be going to the shrink, and the daughter refuses. Maybe the daughter wants to be more independent, and start doing things on her own, but the mom won't let her and the daughter says, But Mom, I'm not a child anymore, and the mom says, Crystal, I don't care how old you are, you can't go around with your shirt off, and Crystal says, I hate wearing shirts. How come boys can walk around with their shirts off and girls can't? And the mother looks tired and says, I don't know, Crystal, but those are the rules. Yeah, well, Dad says rules are made to be broken, says Crystal. And her mother speeds up the car and says, How dare you mention your father at a time like this?

So I went in there and I was definitely not in the mood. I don't know. I think everything is starting to annoy me. I decided to try to get Dr. LaRue mad at me. Actually I didn't really plan for it to happen, it just did.

"So how have you been, Jonah?" Dr. LaRue said.

"Peachy," I said. "I mean, wow, could things be better? I don't think so."

"It must be hard, being back in Pompano, repeating eleventh grade."

"Hard? No, it's great. I love eleventh grade! I'm hoping they'll hold me back next year, too, so I can take it a third time," I said.

I know, I was being really obnoxious.

"How are things with your mother?"

"Mom? Oh, she's great. They've just cast her to play the part of herself in the movie they're making of her life."

"Mm-hmm. And your father? How are things with him?" Dr. LaRue said, twiddling his little mustache.

"I haven't heard from Dad since I got down here. I think he's out of the country. They're going to blast him into outer space again in a couple months though. You know he works for NASA."

I couldn't believe myself. Dr. LaRue knows Dad is in real estate.

"Your mother is the radio personality?"

"Yes. *Dr.* Judith Black. Author of the bestseller *Hello Penis! Hello Vagina!*"

"And how do you feel about her success?" he asked.

"It's great," I enthused. "Mom is a genius."

"Does she know what happened to you at boarding school?"

"Oh, sure. She knows all about it. She's proud of me," I said, beaming like an idiot.

"Are you proud of yourself, Jonah?" Dr. LaRue asked me.

"Proud? Definitely! Did you know that when I was up there I won a pie-eating contest? It's true."

"What else did you do to be proud of?"

"Well, this one time I hit a baseball so hard it knocked out the window of a low-flying airplane, and there was a hijacker holding a gun to the pilot's head and my baseball knocked the gun out of his hand and saved everybody's lives. I'm proud of that, definitely. I mean, it's not like I did it on purpose or anything, but I did it." I couldn't stop myself. I was just babbling like a lunatic.

"Anything else, Jonah?" Dr. LaRue said patiently. He looked at the clock.

There was plenty of time left. So I kept on babbling. And no matter what I said, nothing seemed to get him angry. I kept telling bigger and bigger lies, and it didn't make any difference.

Toward the end of the hour, he said, "So is there anything you regret about your time in Pennsylvania?"

I was just about to tell him how I never got to eat the World's Largest Pretzel, which is in Littiz, PA, but instead I suddenly see Sophie sitting where Dr. LaRue is sitting and she's wearing a yellow sundress and her red fishing hat, the same thing she was wearing the very last time I saw her.

She looks like she's been crying and she leans toward me and whispers, "Don't tell them, okay? Not ever."

"I won't," I promise.

Dr. LaRue fingered his mustache. Then he leaned back in his chair and clasped his fingers around his bald head.

"What?" I said, after he'd been staring at me for a whole minute.

"You said, 'I won't,' Jonah. What question are you answering?"

"I'm not answering any question," I said.

"Well, you can say that again," Dr. LaRue said, finally sounding a little irritated. "What do you think we're doing here, anyway?"

"I don't know," I said.

"Do you think we're just here to blow the hour?"

I guess he knew I'd been lying my head off.

"Dr. LaRue, I'm here because I got kicked out of boarding school and now everyone thinks I'm insane. Which I'm not," I said.

"I see. So you don't have any problems, then. You're pretty well adjusted?" he said.

"I guess."

"Are you happy, Jonah?" he asked me.

"What?"

"I said, are you happy?"

My voice kind of stuck in my throat. Dr. LaRue looked at the clock.

"Time's up," he said.

Sept. 22, 9:15 P.M.

I'm lying here waiting for Honey to finish putting on her makeup so she can drive us both over to the party at Luna's.

There is an amazing silence in our house right now. It's sort of like being at the orchestra and watching the conductor come out and that moment when he raises the baton and stands there looking at the musicians for a second and you know the moment he moves his hand the music will begin but for just that instant nothing has happened yet and all of the music is still in the future.

I can hear the water running in the bathroom. Honey is singing to herself while she gets ready. In the distance I can hear the television on in my mother's room. Probably Lifetime, her favorite channel. Now

—— ■ ——

Honey has turned off the faucet and I can hear it dripping.

A boat is approaching on Cocoabutter Creek, an inboard, I think. I can hear the filter for the pool grinding away in the garage, and the water in the pool lapping through the skimmer.

Cars are roaring up and down Highway 1 five blocks away. There's a jet plane crossing the sky. A dog is barking a few houses down. My clock beside my bed is ticking. It sounds loud.

Now the bathroom door is opening and Honey is coming down the hall to her room and I know she's just put on huge stomping platform shoes because I can hear her clomping around in them even though the whole house has wall-to-wall carpeting. Now she's coming down the

Sept. 23, 2:32 A.M.

We're back. Now Honey is in the bathroom again with the water running, but this time she's taking her makeup off.

Here's what happened. We got in Honey's Jeep and drove over to Luna's. Honey's Jeep is like Honey in a nutshell. I love it. It's this black shiny Wrangler and she almost never puts the top on it. She takes good care of the car, but it also has these weird little touches, like a decapitated dolls' head that hangs off the rearview mirror.

The fact that she has this cool car drives me slightly crazy, even though I know that Mom and Dad would get me a car, too, if I ever got my license back. But just sitting in the car with Honey made me think about how I lost my license, and that made me think about Sophie and that jerk Sullivan and Masthead and the whole messed-up situation. So I closed my eyes and tried to relax. I was feeling a little nervous about this party anyway, and thinking about what happened at the end of last year didn't help.

Honey was quiet during the drive over. She had the radio on but I don't think she was listening to it. She seemed deep in thought, which shouldn't be that rare for a genius like her, but Honey's intelligence always seems to be on the outside, not the inside, if that makes any sense.

Just as we turned onto Luna's street, Honey turned to me and said, "So, Jonah. Let me ask you something."

"Yeah?"

"Are you happy?" she said.

Jesus. Suddenly everyone in Pompano Beach wants to know how happy I am.

"Am I what?" I said. I really didn't feel like having this conversation.

"Happy. Satisfied. Characterized by pleasure, contentedness, or gladness."

"You're really asking me this?"

"Yeah, maybe I am. What's the answer?" Honey insisted.

"I don't know," I said, annoyed. I mean does

everyone want me to walk around with a great big smile on my face all the time?

"Yeah? That's too bad. We gotta do something about that."

"Like what?"

"I'm working on it," Honey said.

"What about you?" I said. "Are you happy?" I asked her.

Honey didn't answer.

As she drove, I took a good look at my sister. She was wearing a black vinyl miniskirt and a ripped black tank top with a big blue star printed on the front of it. Her hair is dark brown but she keeps it dyed black and it's cut in shaggy layers around her face. People don't really lie out to get tan here, but everyone is fairly tan anyway. Except Honey. Her skin is so white it's practically translucent, and it's completely flawless except for one big chicken pox scar on her forehead. She could be pretty, beautiful even, if she didn't scowl so much, and if she didn't have such dark circles under her eyes. And her body is pretty bony, even though she eats a whole box of Ring Dings every day.

Honey's all right, I guess. But happy? She didn't look happy.

We got there and Honey parked behind a long line of cars and checked out her reflection in the

Jeep's side mirror. "Come on, Jonah. It's time to *get* happy," she said.

Actually it's time for me to get some sleep. I will tell the rest of this story tomorrow. Good night.

(Still Sept. 23, 9:30 A.M.)

Saturday morning and no school. I'm eating breakfast out by the pool. Cap'n Crunch. So here's the rest of what happened at Luna's:

Luna lives in Deerfield Beach in a big one-story house with crazy views. The ocean is right in her backyard, the Intercoastal Waterway is out front, and a monster yacht is moored at her dock.

I started to head toward the front entrance but Honey pointed to a basement door and I followed her. Of course, Honey had been to parties there before. She's been everywhere.

The basement was dark, lit only by candles. It was decorated like a hotel lobby or something, with lots of couches and armchairs and oriental rugs and potted plants. Fatboy Slim was on the stereo.

"The wine cellar's down here," Honey explained. Apparently Luna's parents are pretty liberal about her having drinking parties, in their own twisted way. They wouldn't buy their daughter a keg for her parties, or hard alcohol, but they don't see anything wrong with us drinking wine, as long as it's really good wine. This was kind of a waste, I think, since the wine that I usually drink comes in a bottle with a screw cap, not that I drink much wine anyway.

We went over to the table where there were all these uncorked bottles of prime vintage and poured ourselves some. People kept saying hi to my sister, which seriously pissed me off. It was like a reminder to me of how unfair the universe is. I'm the invisible man, and she's like Madame Connected.

Smacky Platte came up to Honey and said, "Yo."

"Yo," my sister said back.

The three of us stood there for a moment, sipping our wine. Then Honey turned to me and said, "I'll catch up with you later, Bro. We're going to go check out the shelter." Then she and Smacky walked off together and went through a door that looked like it led to a long, dark hallway.

I was thinking, *What's the shelter?*

Then these two girls came up to me, one of whom I sort of recognized from my junior history class.

"Hi, you're Jonah Black, aren't you?" said the one I thought I knew. She had thin strawberry blond hair and a freckly nose. There were big spaces between her teeth, as if she still had her baby teeth.

"Yeah, I'm Jonah," I said.

"I'm Brady Walsh," she said, "and this is Lauren Hoogs."

Lauren blushed. She was only about four feet tall.

"I'm in Miss Tenuda's class with you," said Brady.

"Right," I said. "You're a junior," I said, stating the obvious.

"Lauren's a sophomore," Brady said, and they both giggled like they were nervous about talking to me. That kind of made me feel good, or maybe it was just the wine.

"You're friends with that girl Posie Hoff?" Lauren said. The way she said Posie's name made it sound like she was talking about a celebrity.

And now that I think about it, I can see why Posie would be idolized by the other girls at school. She's gorgeous, but not in a fussy, phony way—she just rolls out of bed beautiful. She's genuinely sweet to everyone, but she's not too perky and loud about it—she's just considerate. She has a wicked sense of humor. She can act like a guy—swearing and chewing tobacco and playing with fireworks, but she's also really poised and graceful and womanly. Plus, she has the whole surfer wahine chick thing going, which is beyond cool. Seriously, Posie has got to be the coolest girl in the universe.

"Yeah," I said, feeling like the luckiest person in

the world all of a sudden. "I've known Posie since I was little."

"Wow," Lauren said.

"I've known Lauren since I was two," said Brady.

"Yeah," I said. "It's nice to have friends like that, isn't it? People who know you so well you don't have to explain everything to them all the time."

"Definitely," Lauren said.

"Isn't Posie going out with that guy Wailer now?" Brady asked.

"Yeah," Lauren said, like she knew everything there was to know about Posie. If there was a VH-1 *Behind the Music* with Posie Hoff, Lauren would have taped it and watched it every day.

Lauren and Brady looked at each other and wrinkled up their noses. "Ewwwwww!" they said in unison.

"Hey," I said. "What's so wrong with Wailer?" It was funny—I don't like Wailer, either, but I felt like they were cutting down Posie when they made fun of him.

"Ick," Lauren said. "He is so gross!"

"*Oohhh, Brady*," Brady said, in this big-dumb-guy voice that actually sounded a lot like Wailer. "I wanna play badminton with you, and get married, and live on the beach, and make babies!"

"*Oohhh, Lauren*," Lauren said, and her Wailer

was even better. "I wanna play volleyball with you, and get married, and live on the beach, and make babies!"

Brady and Lauren were practically falling over each other now laughing. "*Oohhh, Jonah,* we wanna join the diving team with you and get married and live on the beach and make babies!" they squealed.

I didn't think this was funny at all.

Lauren tried to stop laughing and took a sip of wine, but then she snorted and the wine came out her nose. She covered her nose with her hand and then she hiccupped so loud that people on the other side of the room looked at her.

"I'm sorry," Brady said. "I think I'd better take her outside." She led her friend outside, both of them still laughing.

I stood there thinking about what they'd said, and wondering if Wailer could really be that gross. Then I realized I was standing alone in the middle of a crowded room, like an idiot. I looked around for Cheese Girl, but she wasn't there, so I sat down on a couch with some girls I used to know, Cecily LaChoy and Shanique O'Reilly. They are both seniors, but Cecily is in the junior German class because she's only been taking it for a year.

Don Shula is like the only school in the world where you'd find a Chinese-French-Belizean girl talking to a West African–Irish girl, and be able to sit down and converse with them in German. It's a crazy world we live in.

"So are you glad to be back?" Cecily asked me.

"Yeah. Pretty much," I said.

"It must have been weird to be so far away from the ocean. I don't think I could handle that," Cecily said.

Shanique wrinkled her nose. "Me neither," she said.

"Yeah," I agreed, although I hadn't really missed the ocean until I came back and saw it and realized how much I missed it. "But I mostly missed my friends," I said.

"Posie Hoff," Cecily said, with the same note of reverence in her voice that Lauren had had.

"Yeah," I said.

"What's she like?" Shanique said. And again I got the feeling that Posie is the girl all the other girls in my school are totally in awe of.

I thought about the night Posie had taken me out to see the phosphorescent jellyfish. And I wanted to say, *Posie is someone who can take a totally ordinary moment and turn it into something you'll remember for the rest of your life*. All of a sudden I had this huge craving for Posie, like I couldn't wait to see her again. I was thinking, *Hey, why shouldn't I go out with Posie?* It was like Pops Berman said, you have to love somebody, why not someone who likes you? Why not your best friend?

Then I remembered why not.

"Posie," I said. "She's fine. She's going out with Wailer. I guess you know."

Shanique and Cecily looked at each other and started giggling.

"What's so funny?" I said. It was like a repeat performance of my conversation with Brady and Lauren.

Shanique said in German, "Ach, Ich mag auf der Beach mit dir leben—"

"Und Babies machen!!!" Cecily squealed.

I couldn't believe it. "How do you guys know Wailer's pickup line?" I said, in English.

Shanique and Cecily stopped laughing. They looked a little embarrassed.

I was feeling pretty angry at this point. Angry at Wailer, and angry at Posie for not seeing through this guy who everyone else in the school knows is a total player. But I still felt like I had to defend her somehow.

"Yeah, well, I think it might be different this time," I said quietly. "I think they're really in love."

I think Cecily could tell I was ready to change the subject.

"So when's your first diving meet?" she asked.

We talked this way for a while and then Thorne came in with Wailer. Cecily and Shanique looked at me and stood up. "See you later, Jonah," they said in unison.

Wailer and Thorne came over to where I was sitting.

"Jonah, my man," Thorne said, raising his glass. "Drinking some vino!"

We clinked glasses.

Wailer was watching Shanique as she walked away. She's got kind of a big chest, and a very muscular-looking butt. She was wearing a thong, too. I could tell.

"Dude," he said. "Check it."

"Hey, Wailer," I said. "How's surfing?"

"Excellent!" he said, brightening up like a lava lamp. "Waves've been awesome all week. You should check it out, Jonah. Why don't you surf, man, if you dive?"

I could have sworn we'd already had this conversation, but I don't think Wailer's long-term memory is very good.

"I don't know. Diving's more fun for me, maybe?" I said.

"Diving?" said Wailer, like it was a bad word. "More fun than surfing? Yeah, right."

"Well, you're good at surfing," I said, trying to be nice. "Posie's pretty good, too."

"Good?" he said, as if I didn't know anything. "Dude! You look at Posie surfing and you understand the whole connection of the earth, the moon, and the ocean. A chick like that, she's just totally one with the universe. It's like she *is* the wave. She just slips into the shoulder of the gnarliest curler and it's like music, man!"

He was getting excited. He looked like he wanted to grab a vine and swing from it, like Tarzan.

"Man, you gotta try it," he said.

"I have tried it, Wailer. I just fall off the board. I don't know. I like diving. I like the power of it, and the speed. It's like I'm conquering the water," I explained.

Thorne took a big gulp of his wine and laughed. "Conquering the water!"

But Wailer looked angry. "You don't conquer water, man! You accept it! It's not about conquering, man! That's so freakin' bogus!"

"It's just the way I look at it, Wailer."

"Well, it's a bad attitude," he scoffed. "Like you're King Kong trying to crush the ocean's banana."

I thought this was pretty funny since Wailer was the one who looked like he ate a lot of bananas.

"It's not an attitude. It's just something I can do well," I said. "I don't like surfing because I'm not any good at it, that's all."

But Wailer wasn't really listening anymore. He was looking across the room, where Shanique was talking to another girl I didn't know. I glanced around the room, suddenly wondering if Watches Boys Dive was going to be there.

"Hey, have you guys ever seen this girl," I said, "I think she's Native American? Long straight black hair. Big brown eyes. Kind of quiet and serious-looking? She comes to swim practice every day."

Wailer didn't hear me. Thorne looked interested, though.

"I don't know who you're talking about, man. You say there's some Indian chick who's got the hots for Jonah Black?"

"I don't know," I said.

Thorne followed Wailer's gaze. He was still staring at Shanique's butt.

"Hey, Wailer," Thorne said. "You want to know a secret about Shanique?"

"Absolutely," said Wailer.

"Squeaking balloons drive her crazy. I mean, *insane.* It's like her Achilles' heel. You want something from her, all you need is a balloon," Thorne said.

Wailer smiled. "A balloon?" he said. "Hell, man, I got a balloon in my car."

Thorne glanced at me. I could tell he was up to something.

"So," I said to Wailer. "I hear you're trying to get Posie to drop out of school, go pro."

"Yeah, maybe," Wailer muttered, distracted.

"Live on the beach and make babies. Is that what you told her?" I said. My heart was speeding up. I was about to pick a fight.

But Wailer didn't hear a thing. "Hey, man. I'll be right back," he said, heading for the door.

"You don't think he's going to his car," I said. "I mean, right this second, so he can get that balloon?"

"I think you can count on it," Thorne said, shaking his head.

"You know what I've been thinking?" I asked him.

"I think I do," Thorne said, clapping me on the back. "Jonah, my friend, I think you're thinking that Wailer must die. Am I right?"

I nodded. "That's exactly what I was thinking."

"Hey, you want to know something?" Thorne said.

"What?"

"I just made up that thing about the balloon. You know, for kicks," he said. "If he really tries to squeak that balloon at Shanique she's going to think he's completely psycho."

I laughed. Suddenly I remembered why Thorne is my best friend.

Thorne smiled and clinked glasses with me

again. "Hey, I haven't forgotten about finding that chick's number for you, okay? I'm working on it."

"Okay," I said.

I saw this girl Dell Merriwether heading in our direction. Thorne reached into his pocket and pulled out a pair of glasses. I frowned at him. Thorne doesn't wear glasses.

"Thorne?" I said. "You have problems with your eyesight now?"

He smiled. "It's clear glass," he said, putting them on. "I had them made."

"What for?"

Thorne looked at me like I was stupid. "Jonah, you were never in the Boy Scouts, were you?"

"What's that supposed to mean?" I said.

He whispered, "Be prepared, dude!"

Dell Merriwether came up to us. "How's it going, Woodman?" she said to Thorne.

"Outstanding, Miss M!" Thorne said, grinning. "Hey, I read that Dostoyevsky you gave me. Those Brothers K are out of control!"

"I thought you'd get into that," Dell said. "I knew it. When I finished the book I was like, whoa, Thorne is going to be all over this."

"So do you want to talk about it? There's this one part in the story where I was like, hey, what's this about?" Thorne said. Good old Thorne.

"Sure," Dell said, "if Jonah doesn't mind." She looked at me and smiled. "Have you ever read Dostoyevsky, Jonah?"

"No," I said. "Not yet."

Thorne winked at me. "You should, man. Literature's important!"

The little book club walked outside. As they went through the door, Thorne gave me the thumbs-up sign. I couldn't believe how he'd transformed himself into Mr. English Professor in like, two seconds. Then I remembered what he'd said about the Boy Scouts, and wondered what else he had merit badges for besides literature.

Right after they left, Donna, my Cheese Girl, walked in. Her face lit up when she saw me. I think my face lit up, too. As she walked across the room toward me, I could tell she'd been drinking.

Speaking of drinking, I have a major headache. I think I'm going to leave this for a while and go for a swim.

(Still Sept. 23, a few hours later.)

Okay, I'm back. Mom and Honey are at the Coral Springs Mall, looking for clothes. That should be interesting. Honey in Ann Taylor, Mom in Rampage. So now it's just me at home, down by the dock.

Back to last night.

So Donna was all drunk, and she came right up to me and sat down in a heap like it was this huge effort, getting there.

"How's it going, Donna?" I said.

"Honeshtly, Jonah?" she slurred. "I'm pretty drunk."

She leaned her head on my shoulder. Her hair smelled like cigarette smoke.

"Are you okay?" I said.

"Hey, Jonah, is it okay if I tell you something?" she asked.

"Sure," I said. "It's okay."

Donna hiccupped into her hand. "It's kind of personal," she said.

"It's okay," I said.

Her earring was pressing into my shoulder, but it felt nice sitting with her like that.

"Okay," she said. "So, it's like, I mean . . ."

She stopped talking and closed her eyes.

"What, Donna?" I said. "What's wrong?"

"It's . . ." she said, her eyes still closed.

"It's okay, you can tell me," I said, kind of hugging her shoulders.

Donna shook her head and closed her mouth up tight. Then she lurched forward and threw up on the floor.

"Ugh," she gasped. "I'm sorry."

I rubbed her back a little. "It's okay," I said. "Don't worry about it."

Donna didn't look at me. She just stood up and stumbled toward the door, running outside to where all the cars were parked. I started to follow her, but it was dark and I couldn't see where she went. Then I saw a VW Jetta roar off down the street. And all I could think was, I hope that wasn't her. She was way too messed up to drive.

It's pretty sad when I think about it now. The only girl that's interested in me suddenly blows chunks.

There was no one else around that I knew, so I went over to the door Honey and Smacky had gone through earlier, thinking I'd try to find Posie. The door led to a long, narrow cement hallway that sloped downhill. At the end of the hallway was a heavy door, almost like the door of a bank vault. I pushed it open.

Now I knew why Honey had called that room "the shelter." Luna has a bomb shelter in her house! It's crazy.

A single blue lightbulb hung down from a wire in the ceiling, barely lighting the room, and a haze of smoke hung thick in the air. There were mattresses all over the floor and couples were lying all over them, making out. Some of the couples were doing more than that, so it was lucky the room was so dark. In one corner were Link Zolot and Amanda Brasier, sucking each other's faces off. My sweet sister, Honey, was with Smacky, smoking a big roll-up next to a metal drum marked CIVIL DEFENSE. Over by a stack of tomato soup cans were Joe Dalanzo and Nuala Blake, who had her shirt off. Posie was sitting up, with Wailer's head in her lap. I guess he never found that balloon after all. Anyway, all together there were about twenty people there, lying all over each other in the Hayes family bomb shelter.

The only person who wasn't with someone, besides me, was Luna herself. She was sitting all alone next to the stereo, playing Moby. She looked sad.

"Hi, Jonah," she said.

"Hey, Luna. Nice party," I said.

She shrugged, not saying anything. She looked like she was about to cry.

"Are you okay?" I said.

She looked around the shelter and then up at me. "Do you want to get out of here and talk?" she said. "I really want to talk to you."

I remembered the story Thorne had told me about Luna in the fire station. It sounded like Luna was pretty loose. I wondered if she only wanted to talk, but then I figured if she wanted to fool around, we wouldn't be leaving the shelter. Luna stood up and I followed her out into that dark, narrow hallway.

Suddenly she turns around and puts her arms around my neck and kisses me. Her hands are moving like spiders over me as she unbuttons first my shirt and then hers. She pulls my head down so I can kiss her neck. Her skin tastes like the alcohol in her perfume. Poison. She slides her hand into my jeans and the ground starts to rumble beneath us. There is a bright flash of light from outside. Too late, I realize a nuclear bomb has been dropped, and we aren't even inside the shelter. We begin to run toward the heavy door to the shelter but we trip on our clothes and Sophie cries, "Jonah, stop. I don't care anymore." She hugs me close and I kiss her as hard as I can as the two of us turn into vapor. I don't even mind becoming mist as long as I am with her. I can smell glycerin soap and lavender and smoke and as we disappear I tell her, "We don't ever have to go back. We'll stay like this forever."

I followed Luna back out to the basement and we sat down on a couch. There wasn't any music on now. Luna poured me a glass of wine and handed it to me. "I'm so glad you found me," she said.

I took a sip of wine. "Are you okay? You looked upset."

Luna gathered her curly brown hair up in her

hands, pulled it up on top of her head, and let it fall. She sighed tiredly. "Oh, I'm just being a stupid girl. You don't want to hear about it."

"That's okay," I said. "You can tell me."

She moved closer to me on the couch and put her head on my shoulder, just like Donna had done. And I was thinking, *Okay, just please don't throw up.*

"Well," Luna said. "I guess my main problem is that I have this huge crush. It's like all I think about." She started fiddling with one of the buttons on my shirt. "I know it sounds crazy, but I spend all my time daydreaming. I don't even know what's real anymore."

"I think I know what you mean, Luna," I said.

"Really? Is that true or are you just saying that?" she asked me.

"It's true," I told her. "I think I daydream a lot, too."

Luna wrapped her arms around my waist and hugged me. Her head was still on my shoulder. Actually, by this time it was kind of resting on my chest.

"I knew you'd understand," she said. "I knew you'd be the one person I could talk to."

I just sat there holding her, not sure where this was going.

"So will you talk to him? Do you think you could

find out for me if he still likes me? After we had sex it was like he didn't want to talk to me anymore. I was just like, hello?" Luna said. She started to cry into my shirt. "I mean, I know Thorne has a reputation, but I really thought we were different. I'm so in love with him."

I didn't know what to say. I knew Thorne was off somewhere fooling around with Dell Merriwether as the two of them discussed Russian novels.

"I'll try," I said, just to be nice. I felt really bad for Luna.

"Oh, thank you, Jonah," Luna said.

She shifted herself in my arms and tilted her face up to mine. Then all of a sudden she kissed me. Her lips tasted like tears and wine and it felt nice, but I didn't want to be kissing Luna Hayes, especially not after what she'd said about being so in love with Thorne.

I pulled my head away. Luna didn't even seem to mind. She just went back to sitting with her head on my shoulder.

"Have you ever felt like you've met the one person you're destined to be with?" she sighed. "What am I saying? I know guys don't think like this."

"That's not true," I said. "Some guys think like that."

I wondered what Sophie was doing, right at that

exact second. Was she at some party at Masthead, drinking wine? Was she alone?

Then Thorne and Dell came in from outside, and there was absolutely no doubt that they had just had sex. They oozed through the basement with their hair all mussed up, happy smiles on their faces, carrying their empty glasses back to the table for more wine.

"Hi, Luna," Dell said as they passed us on their way to the bomb shelter.

Thorne winked at me.

Luna started crying again. "It's no good living in your imagination," she said. Then she stood up, kissed me on the cheek, and walked resolutely toward the stairs.

I didn't know what to do, so I got up and walked back into the bomb shelter.

Wailer and Posie were still in the corner together. It was depressing. I couldn't even face trying to talk to her. All I could think was, I hope Pops and Lauren Hoogs and Cecily LaChoy are all wrong about Wailer. I hope I'm wrong, too.

I sat down on the edge of a mattress and looked at a pile of CDs on the floor. Someone came and sat down next to me. It was my sister.

"Hello, Newman," she said.

"Hey," I said. "Some party, huh?"

"Brotherman," said Honey. "You need some serious help."

"You think?" I said.

"I know," Honey said. "Sitting in the corner? All by yourself?"

"I don't really mind," I said. "I'm having a good time."

"But you could be having a truly great time," Honey said.

She looked over at Wailer and Posie. They were rocking from side to side, holding each other and kissing.

"I think I know what you need," Honey said quietly.

"Honey," I said, tiredly. "I don't want you to hook me up with some random girl, okay? I really don't."

"Okay," Honey said. She laughed. "Poor little Jonah. No wonder you're only in eleventh grade."

I didn't even have the energy to get mad at her. I was thinking about what I could do to Wailer, like maybe put superglue on his surfboard so he'd get stuck and float off into the ocean and fall into a pool of stinging jellyfish. A pool of phosphorescent Portuguese man-of-wars, just suspended in the water like killer clouds.

AMERICA ONLINE INSTANT MESSAGE
9-24, 5:37 P.M.

NORTHGIRL999: Hello Jonah is that you?

JBLACK94710: Aine? How are you?

NORTHGIRL999: I am fine. I am so sorry I had to log off before. You must have thought rude girl!

JBLACK94710: I thought I must have pissed you off somehow.

NORTHGIRL999: pissed off? What is pissed off?

JBLACK94710: I thought I made you angry.

NORTHGIRL999: no, no. I loved talking to you. You make so funny!

JBLACK94710: what happened?

NORTHGIRL999: my boyfriend woke up. He would not have been funny to see me talk with you to computer!

JBLACK94710: your boyfriend? I thought you had a fight with him.

NORTHGIRL999: I did. That is why I talked to you on computer. I did not wish to sleep next to him after that.

JBLACK94710: you mean he was sleeping right there?

NORTHGIRL999: yes. And I was already starting to cyber, Jonah. I had my shirt off. He was one angry bear Jonah!

JBLACK94710: really?

NORTHGIRL999: yes Jonah I told you before I have big

—■—

crush on you. Your diving board photo is so hot!

JBLACK94710: well you are very pretty Aine. But you don't need me to tell you that.

NORTHGIRL999: I like it for you to say.

JBLACK94710: well you are. I wish you didn't live in Norway!

NORTHGIRL999: oh you would love Norway if you came to visit we could take sauna—make love in sauna.

JBLACK94710: won't it be too hot?

NORTHGIRL999: oh, you are so American! Sauna is like religion here. You sit in sauna and the world goes good-bye.

JBLACK94710: sounds great.

NORTHGIRL999: drink champagne and jump out of sauna and roll in snow and then back in sauna and make love. Oh how I would love you Jonah Black in sauna!

JBLACK94710: I think I would like that too Aine. This is very weird though. Can you tell me more about yourself so I can get a picture of you?

NORTHGIRL999: you have picture of me! Oh wait I have new picture I will send it now.

JBLACK94710: That's not what I meant.

NORTHGIRL999: Is it there?

JBLACK94710: it's arriving now. Hang on while I open it.

JBLACK94710: oh my God.

NORTHGIRL999: you like?

<u>JBLACK94710:</u> oh my God.

<u>JBLACK94710:</u> what are you sitting on? It looks like some sort of

<u>NORTHGIRL999:</u> is polar bear rug. Very soft for love. :)

<u>JBLACK94710:</u> is that your house?

<u>NORTHGIRL999:</u> is our summer house. There is fireplace there with polar bear rug in front.

<u>JBLACK94710:</u> I think it might be too hot for you if you came here to Florida. No one has rugs like that here.

<u>NORTHGIRL999:</u> I would love Florida. Are you near from Disney World? I always want to go to Disney World.

<u>JBLACK94710:</u> you should come. I could show you around.

<u>NORTHGIRL999:</u> do you miss Pennsylvania? Did you like it there?

<u>JBLACK94710:</u> I miss it sometimes.

<u>NORTHGIRL999:</u> did you have girlfriend there?

<u>NORTHGIRL999:</u> are you still there?

<u>NORTHGIRL999:</u> Jonah?

<u>JBLACK94710:</u> there was a girl that I loved very much. I don't know if you could call her my girlfriend.

<u>NORTHGIRL999:</u> what was this girlfriend name?

<u>JBLACK94710:</u> Sophie.

<u>NORTHGIRL999:</u> what was she like?

<u>JBLACK94710:</u> just sitting next to her in the library was like this giant adventure.

<u>NORTHGIRL999:</u> What did she look like?

<u>JBLACK94710:</u> Dark blond hair. Blue eyes. Delicate. Like snow.

<u>NORTHGIRL999:</u> does she know you love her Jonah?

<u>JBLACK94710:</u> she should.

<u>NORTHGIRL999:</u> but did you ever tell her?

<u>JBLACK94710:</u> I saved her.

<u>NORTHGIRL999:</u> how?

<u>JBLACK94710:</u> I gave up everything. I wound up back in Pompano Beach in 11th grade for her.

<u>NORTHGIRL999:</u> does she know what you did for her?

<u>JBLACK94710:</u> I don't know.

<u>NORTHGIRL999:</u> so you did not tell her?

<u>NORTHGIRL999:</u> Jonah?

<u>NORTHGIRL999:</u> Jonah?

GOODBYE FROM AMERICA ONLINE!
YOU HAVE SPENT 17 MINUTES ONLINE.
YOUR PRICING PLAN THIS MONTH
CALLS FOR UNLIMITED USAGE.

— ■ —

Governor, State of Florida
Governor's Office,
The Capitol,
Tallahassee, FL 32399
September 24

Dear Governor:

My name is Jonah Black and I am writing to you today to request that you make me a senior at Don Shula High School, in Pompano Beach. I attended ninth grade at Don Shula and then I went for tenth and eleventh grades to Masthead Academy, which is in Bryn Mawr, Pennsylvania. I went there because it is near my father's house and he thought it would be good for me to go to a school like Masthead. Unfortunately I had to leave Masthead at the end of my junior year as a result of a complicated situation which I won't go in to now. The point is that I finished eleventh grade and I deserve to be a senior. However, Mrs. Perella, the vice principal at Don Shula, says that I didn't finish my junior year in good standing. This is not true.

I did have to withdraw from Masthead before I'd taken all of my final exams, but I passed everything anyway. I think the big issue is that I got a D in German there, which is what has Mrs. Perella all upset because Don Shula is supposed to be a magnet school for languages, so I've been held back. But I was getting an A in almost all my other classes at Masthead, and I would have done better in German if I had been able to take the final.

I hope you can understand what an injustice this is. Repeating eleventh grade again is a horrible punishment, almost the same as sending me to the electric chair for something I didn't do. I know you have signed pardons for people who have been put to death. Well, this is almost the same thing. I think I deserve a second chance. If you'll pardon me I promise that when I graduate I will be an upstanding citizen of the state of Florida.

I am looking forward to hearing from you.

God bless America.

Sincerely,

Jonah Black

PS. You should know that my younger sister, Honey, is a senior this year, because she's a genius, and skipped a grade. I am not saying she should be put back, I'm only saying that to have your little sister a grade ahead of you is pretty humiliating, as I'm sure you can imagine.

PPS. I wrote our school principal, Dr. Chamberlin, about the situation, but he didn't write back. Do you know if he exists?

> ### Sept. 27

Okay, I had a totally wack session with Dr. LaRue today. He asked me all these weird hypothetical questions. I'm serious, some of them were really strange, like, "If you could be any kind of food, what would you be?"

I said, "Cheese."

"If you were a kind of disease, what disease would you be?"

I said, "Chicken pox."

"If you were a kind of car, what kind of car would you be?"

I thought about it for a moment. "A BMW."

"It's snowing. Your mother asks you to pick up some coffee. What do you do?"

"It's not going to be snowing in Florida," I said.

"Humor me."

"I go out and get it for her but maybe while I'm out I go and do something else I think is fun, like I go down to the ocean and watch my friend Posie surf. Then I come back, just in time for Mom to begin worrying about me. Except she doesn't even notice that I'm gone," I said.

"You find five dollars on the street while walking home. What do you do with it?"

"I buy flowers for Posie and stick them in her mailbox and take off without letting her know who they're from," I said. It was such a good idea I thought I might do it anyway, just for fun.

"You're traveling on a one-lane road and you're stuck behind a slow-moving van. You get to a place where you can pass the van and you pull into the other lane. Just as you're about to draw even with the van, it starts to blink, indicating it's going to turn left, crossing the lane you're in. What do you do?"

"What am I driving?" I asked.

"A BMW."

"I floor the Beamer and pass him just before he hits me," I said.

"Even though that could cause an accident?"

I shrugged. "I'd be okay."

"You come to a four-way stop and three cars

arrive at the intersection simultaneously. Which car goes first?"

"What is this, a driving test?" I said.

"Which car?"

"I don't know. I guess I kind of check out the other drivers and if they look like they don't know what's happening, I just sort of go." I knew there were specific guidelines for this in the driver's manual, but I couldn't remember what they were.

"You aren't a very good driver, are you, Jonah?"

"Does that make me a bad person?" I said.

"No. But maybe you're someone that other people shouldn't travel with."

"There's nothing wrong with traveling with me," I protested. "I look out for other people."

"Do you look out for other people better than you look out for yourself?"

"Maybe," I said, wishing he would ask me another question.

"If you could wear any article of girls' clothing, what would it be?"

I was kind of mad about that one. "I already told you, I'm not—"

"Just answer the question."

"Mittens," I told him.

"You see your best friend, Posie, cheating on a math test. Do you tell the teacher?"

I shook my head. "Posie wouldn't cheat on a math test."

"What about—what's his name—Thorne?"

"Okay, Thorne would cheat," I said. "But I wouldn't tell."

"You're a psychiatrist and one of your clients confesses to a murder while you're in a session. Would you contact the police and have your client arrested?"

"Of course not," I said. "That's so bogus."

"What if he'd murdered your friend Thorne?"

"I still wouldn't tell," I insisted.

"What if he'd murdered that girl in Pennsylvania, Sophie?"

"I'd try to warn her in advance," I said. "I'd try to save her."

"What if she's already dead?"

"I'd still try to save her."

"How could you save her if she was already dead?"

"Nobody's so dead you can't save them," I said, even though I knew what I was saying made no sense. After all, our whole conversation made no sense.

"You're a very interesting young man, Jonah. Do you think of yourself as interesting?"

"No," I said.

"Well, it's interesting what these questions show about you. You're a little reckless, if not careless.

You're loyal. You're considerate. And you're bolder than you might think."

"Okay," I said, not sure what to make of all that. "But if you ask me something directly, I'll tell you the truth. I don't like being tricked."

"All right, Jonah," Dr. LaRue said. "From now on I will."

We'll see. He's a tricky little bastard, that shrink.

That's it for today. It's time for mac and cheese and MTV. See, I'm really just a normal kid.

——— ■ ———

Something happened at swim practice today that made me hate Wailer even more. I was doing my usual warm-up routine in the pool, swimming a few laps. Then I stopped and stood up in the shallow end to catch my breath. I looked up at the stands, but Watches Boys Dive wasn't there. So I pulled myself up onto the edge of the pool and just sat there, dangling my feet in the water. I guess I was feeling kind of lonely and sorry for myself.

Then Coach Davis blew the whistle and called us all over.

"Boys," he said. "I want to introduce a new member of the diving team—Wailer Conrad."

I looked up and saw Wailer standing next to Mr. Davis in his little Speedo racing suit. Everybody started to applaud, and I had to applaud, too, because a member of the team is a member of the team. My first thought was *Hello?* I thought Wailer was so against diving. I mean what about all that stuff he was saying at Luna's party about how you don't control the water, you achieve oneness with it or something. And how I was all into crushing the water's banana. And now there we were. Teammates! Jesus.

My second thought was, *Uh-oh. What if he's really good?*

That turned out not to be a problem. Wailer has got to be one of the worst divers I've ever seen. I mean, he has the strength, and he gets enough air. But he doesn't seem to have a sense of coordination or balance, which is weird for someone who's so good on a surfboard. He kept trying these pretty advanced dives for a beginner and he'd just lose his center and crash into the pool on his back. It was kind of painful. He was determined, though, I have to give him credit for that. He didn't give up.

Coach Davis looked like he needed a drink, but he was very patient with Wailer. He even got on the board with him to show him what to do with his arms.

I didn't talk to Wailer at all during practice, but I knew I was going to have to say something. You can't have a block about somebody else on your team or else it's going to bug you all season. Plus, it just didn't make any sense that he was there. I mean, why diving? So finally, when we were in the showers, and we were standing next to each other drying off, and I was trying to come up with something halfway decent to say, Wailer all of a sudden goes, "Hey, Jonah. What do you think of this dude Davis?"

"I think he rocks," I said. "Best coach I ever had."

"Yeah, everybody seems to like him," Wailer said.

We stood there for a while, trying to get the water out of our ears.

"So, Wailer," I said, finally. "You're like, on the team now?"

"Yeah," he said. "Looks like it."

"I didn't know you were into diving. I thought you had the whole—you know, surfing thing going on." I was trying to be polite, but I really wanted to ask him what the hell he thought he was doing.

"Yeah, well, I was talking to my college advisor and she was like, Woodrow, you don't have enough extracurriculars," he explained. "I knew there weren't enough divers on the team, so I thought I'd check it out."

I kind of choked. What an idiot. He didn't care about diving. He was only doing it to improve his record. But what about all that stuff about dropping out and marrying Posie? What did he need extracurriculars for?

"But Wailer," I said. I was trying to keep my voice down so the other guys wouldn't hear us. "At

Luna's party you said diving was stupid. You went on and on about how it wasn't about conquering the water and how surfing was so much better. You were a total jerk about it. Now you're on the team. What's with that?"

"Yeah, well, you gotta do what you gotta do," he said, shrugging his big gorilla shoulders like it was no big deal.

"And I thought you and Posie were dropping out. What do you care about your college record?" I said.

Wailer walked over to his locker and started getting dressed. "Dude, that could work out, or it might not. I gotta cover my bases," he said. "'Course I'm never going to dive like you, man. Everybody says you're like some Olympic guy, or something."

I wondered if Wailer knew how much I wanted him dead.

"Well, maybe if you work at it you could get good, too," I said, and I walked away. It was the most arrogant thing I've ever said in my life. God I was mad.

On my way out I looked for Watches Boys Dive. I wonder if something has happened to her.

Oct. 1

This weird thing just happened. Honey was sitting in the backyard by herself on this rock that overlooks the canal. Suddenly I realized my little sister was crying. Her shoulders were shaking and every now and then she moved her hand to her eyes and anyway she hates the backyard because all the rich people and their yachts just make her angry. And then I thought, *Honey, crying? No way.* But what was she doing out there then? I couldn't figure it out.

So then I did something. I picked up the phone and called Dad. Who, of course, wasn't home. It was Tiffany's voice on the machine: "Leave a message for Dan or Tiffany at the sound of the chime," and I was thinking, *Chime?* And then, cheesy as it sounds, the machine chimed like a doorbell, and I started talking.

—— ■ ——

"Hello, Dad, it's Jonah. I was just calling to check in. Everything is going fine down here. I guess I was just wondering if you could do me a favor and like, call down here once in a while and talk to Honey. I think she really misses you. Um, her birthday is next week, the twelfth, so that would be a good time to call. Actually, she'll probably be going out, so maybe call her the day before. Don't tell her I said you should call or anything. Anyway, that's it. Say hi to Tiffany for me. See ya."

When I hung up the phone, I looked out and Honey wasn't in the backyard anymore. Then I heard this creak out in the hallway and footsteps and I opened the door but no one was there. A minute later I heard the roar of her Jeep out in the street. I'm really hoping Honey didn't hear me, because if she finds out I tried to get Dad to call her she'll kill me. There's nothing she hates more than people being kind to her.

—— ■ ——

Thorne caught up with me after my workout today. I was headed out to my bicycle when he whistled, and there he was, leaning against the hood of his Beetle.

"Your friend, Sophie," he said. "Turns out she's harder to find than I thought."

"Yeah?" I said, pretending I'd forgotten all about him finding her number. Which I definitely haven't.

"No known listing for the parents in any city in Maine. No e-mail addresses. No phones. Even your fancy prep school doesn't have a home address for her."

"You contacted Masthead?" I said, getting panicky.

"Don't worry, they don't suspect anything. I was very professional. I just want you to know I'm working on it. It's a bitch, though. It's like this chick doesn't even exist," he said.

173

I didn't say anything, but I felt my ears getting hot. It pissed me off that he'd say that.

"Blackman, tell me the truth. This chick does exist, right? I mean, you're not trying to get me to find the address of some imaginary friend of yours or something, are you?" he said, laughing.

"Do you think I'd be that stupid?" I said. I was really mad at him.

"I didn't say you're stupid. It's just creepy," Thorne said. "You're sure it's Maine?"

"I'm sure it's Maine. At least, I think so," I said, getting flustered. I mean, what did I know? She could be anywhere. "No. I mean, yes, it's definitely Maine."

Thorne nodded. "Okay. I haven't given up. I'm getting their tax returns from the IRS. That'll have their address."

"How are you getting their tax returns?" I said. I was actually kind of impressed.

Thorne smiled. "You wouldn't believe what you can get," he said.

Wailer came out of the gym and got into his SUV. He waved to us. Only Thorne waved back.

"Hey, Thorne," I said. "You know what we were talking about at Luna's party? About how Wailer must die?"

Thorne nodded. "Yeah," he said. "I remember that."

"Well, how would you do it?" I said. "If you had to kill someone?"

"Ground-up glass in their food," Thorne said, without even stopping to think. "They don't even notice it, but it chews them up inside. No one knows what happened."

Thorne really does have a creepy side to him. It almost sounded like he'd tried the glass thing.

"Well, I'm ready," I said. "I'm sick of Wailer's crap. I just can't believe Posie has totally bought all his lies about—"

Thorne and I said, in unison, "Living on the beach and making babies."

Thorne shook his head. "That is the best line. Chicks go crazy for it." His voice was full of admiration.

"It's crap," I said. "Seriously. We have to expose him."

Thorne snapped out of it when I said that. It was like he'd been struck by lightning.

"Expose him! Absolutely!" he shouted, doing a little drum roll on the hood of his car. "Oh, man, I have all the gear for it. I've got a digital camera. A sonar that can pick up and record cell phones. I think we can put together a whole package, you know, and like, send it to Posie. Wailer won't know what hit him!"

"A package?" I said. "What kind of package?"

"You know, photos of him with some other girl. Tapes of him on the phone feeding her the same bullshit he's been feeding Posie. This is great. Man, Jonah! You and me, we got a project now!"

"What girl has he been with lately?" I said. "Besides Posie?"

"I don't know. We can set him up if we have to. I know plenty of girls who'd like to take a pull on the tail of the Wail." Thorne shook my hand. "Jonah, you're a genius."

I don't feel like a genius. I just don't want my friend Posie getting slimed.

Oct. 3, 12:35 A.M.

I'm about to go to bed but I have to write this down because Honey just pointed out something that kind of freaked me out.

I logged on to AOL before bed to see if Northgirl was on. I felt a little bad about logging off on her the other night. So I tried to send her an Instant Message and I got back "Northgirl999 is not currently signed on." Then Honey opened my door without even knocking.

"What are you doing, Dufus, downloading porno?"

"Yeah, and I saw those pictures of you and a billy goat," I said.

"Ha!" She walked into the room and looked over my shoulder. "So who's Northgirl?"

At first I didn't want to tell her, but I thought she might think it was funny, so I showed her the two Instant Message sessions that I'd saved on the hard drive. Honey stood there reading it all and her face lit right up.

"So who do you think she is?" she said.

"I don't know. Some insane girl from Norway."

Honey just smiled at me. "I'll tell you this, Needlebrain. She could be a lot of people, but she's not from Norway."

"What do you mean? She's a student at the University of Stockholm."

"Stockholm isn't in Norway, genius. It's in Sweden."

"Sweden?" I said. Oops.

"Sweden."

"So, maybe she's a Norwegian girl going to school in Sweden," I said.

"She says right here she's in Norway. Look, she even spelled Stockholm wrong," Honey said.

I looked at the dialog. Honey was right.

"Also, this line here that she claims is in Norwegian." Honey pointed to it. "That's not Norwegian. It's not anything. It's made-up words."

"How do you know?" I already knew but I had to ask.

"Because, Einstein, I speak Norwegian and Swedish," Honey said.

"I know," I snapped at her. I hate that Honey's so smart. It pisses me off. "Well, she doesn't speak English very well, I can tell you that."

"She's only pretending not to be able to speak English," Honey said. "I hate to tell you this, big brother, but the mistakes she's making here? They are totally bogus. No one who speaks Scandinavian languages would make mistakes like that. Face it, this is no Scandinavian chick. It's probably some middle-aged man from Kansas."

I opened the jpeg files that Aine had sent me. "She sent me these. She said this was her."

Honey just laughed. "Oh, you *loser*. This chick is definitely not real. You think a girl who looks like this is going to send you her picture just out of the blue?"

I felt stupid. "I don't know."

Honey thought for a while. "Well, Scrotumface. You got yourself a secret admirer, even if it is a serial killer in a jail cell somewhere."

She looked at me. "What's wrong? You're disappointed?"

I really was disappointed that Northgirl wasn't real. She seemed so real, and she was nice. And now she turns out not to be, just like everything else in my life.

"What am I going to say to her the next time I talk to her?" I asked Honey.

———— ■ ————

"Don't say anything. Just pretend you believe her bullshit. You're having fun, aren't you?" Honey said.

"But it's all lies," I said. "Maybe she is a man from Kansas. Who knows? It's no fun if she's just lying to me."

Honey started to leave. "It's a shame you don't have more of an imagination, big brother," she said. "You might have more fun."

I don't know. I always thought I had a pretty good imagination.

Oct. 7, Saturday

Well, today was pretty fun. Thorne and I were like Sherlock Holmes and Dr. Watson. Thorne was Holmes, of course. I couldn't believe all the stuff he had—digital cameras and mikes and all this spy gear. He said he'd gotten some of it off the Internet and the rest "in barter for other services rendered." Thorne scares me sometimes.

Anyway, we were sitting in Thorne's Beetle just before noon, parked behind the dune where everyone hangs out. Thorne wouldn't tell me what we were waiting for, he just told me to be patient. We'd even bought a box of doughnuts and some Cokes so we could sit there, stuffing our faces like cops at a stakeout.

Then, about half an hour later, Wailer came

———— ■ ————

walking down the beach. He was carrying his surf-board, which he stabbed into the sand so it was standing there like a big tombstone, and then he lay down in the sun with these little plastic sun protectors over his eyes. Thorne put on a pair of headphones and directed this long, skinny mike at Wailer's body. A moment later I heard the sound of Wailer breathing and the waves crashing coming through the car stereo. Thorne hit Record on his tape recorder and handed me the digital camera.

"Okay, now you get him in the frame, and get ready to shoot when his girlfriend gets here," Thorne whispered.

"How do you know he's meeting someone?"

"'Cause I called him up and told him I wanted to meet him here," Thorne said, batting his eyelashes.

"You?"

Thorne held up a small device that said E-SCRAMBLER on the side. He talked through it. It changed his voice so it sounded exactly like a girl's. It was eerie.

"Wow," I said.

"It's got fifty different settings," Thorne said proudly. "It can make you sound like an Australian aborigine or an old man from Brooklyn."

"Who did you say you were?"

"I didn't. I said I was his secret admirer," Thorne said.

"And some girl is going to meet him here? How did you manage that?"

He cleared his throat and imitated Wailer. "Hey, Luna, you wanna do somethin' Saturday? Hang at the beach?" He was good. I'd have fallen for it.

"Luna?" I said. Poor Luna.

So only a few minutes later Luna Hayes came strolling down the beach wearing a white bikini, all ready to hook up with Wailer Conrad. People amaze me sometimes.

"Okay, Jonah, make sure you get them in your viewfinder," Thorne whispered. He was really into it.

I had them right at the crosshairs. We could hear their voices perfectly through the stereo.

"Yo, Luna. What's up?" Wailer said.

"Hey, Wailer." She giggled. "You been surfin'?"

"Yeah. Waves kinda suck today, though. It's wicked flat."

"Yeah," she said. "Maybe they'll get better when the wind picks up a little."

They talked for a while, mostly about surfing and then about this band called the Lemons that's going to play in Ft. Lauderdale next month. I happened to know that Wailer probably can't stand them—they're a total girl band—but he pretended to be really interested. That was the first indication that something was going to happen.

Finally Luna said, "So where's Posie?"

Wailer's lower lip started to protrude. He looked out at the water, trying to act all dramatic. It was like a bad movie.

"Are you okay, Wailer?" Luna said.

"Yeah," he said. "It's just—"

"What?" Luna said, touching his arm.

"I don't know. She's not good about—you know. Listening." He honestly looked like he was about to cry. It was ridiculous.

"I know!" said Luna. "She's so totally into herself! It's like talking to a brick wall."

"Sometimes I'm like . . ." Wailer stammered. "Forget it."

"No, what?" Luna said.

"I can't tell you," Wailer said, crossing his arms over his chest and hugging himself. He's actually not a bad actor.

"Yes, you can," Luna said, rubbing his arm. "You can trust me, Wailer."

"This is hard," Wailer said. "It's really hard to say."

"I'm listening," Luna said soothingly.

"I don't know," Wailer said. "It's like sometimes I don't know if we have the same vision of the future. Like, I mean, Posie wants to go pro, and compete in all these tournaments, and all this other hard-core stuff, you know? And me—all I wanna do is . . ."

Thorne and I looked at each other.

"What is it, Wailer?" Luna said. "What do you want to do?"

"I want to live on the beach. And make babies!"

He covered his face with his hands, like he was crying.

"Wailer," Luna said, kneeling over him. "It's okay. Really."

"You must think I'm stupid," Wailer said, his voice cracking.

"No," Luna said. "It's not stupid. It's beautiful. It's like, my fantasy. I just don't have anybody to . . ."

The two of them looked at each other. Then Wailer leaned in and started kissing her. Even though it seemed inevitable to me, Luna looked like she was taken by surprise. Her back kind of stiffened up. But not for long. A few seconds later, they were rolling around in the sand.

"I gotta remember that line," Thorne said, shaking his head in admiration.

I was so mad at Wailer. He was such a faker. I wanted to jump out of the car and go down there and kill him.

"Don't forget to take the pictures, Jonah," Thorne said.

So I did. We were there for ten more minutes. By the time Wailer had taken Luna's bikini top off, the camera's memory was full. So we left.

Thorne headed over to the IHOP, whistling and singing, all pleased with himself. He was so happy he ordered a giant stack of pancakes with a fried egg on top. I had waffles, but I wasn't very hungry.

"Okay," I said. "So what now?"

"Now," said Thorne. "Now we post this on a Web site. We send Posie the address. She logs on. Bingo, Wailer's doing the dead man's float. God, that was so *easy*!"

I pushed my waffle around in the boysenberry syrup. I thought about Posie looking at the Web site, how she'd feel learning about Wailer that way.

"What?" Thorne said.

"Nothing," I said.

"I don't like the look on your face, Jonah," he said. "You're about to have one of your annoying attacks of morality."

"It's not that," I said. "It's just . . . I'm not so sure I want Posie to find out that way. I mean, she'll be crushed."

"Yeah!" he said, as if this was obvious.

"I don't want to hurt her," I said.

"Jonah?" Thorne said. "This is Posie we're talking about. She'll get over it."

"I don't know, Thorne," I said. "I think she really loves him. This is really going to set her back."

"You want her to keep going out with Wailer? Is that what you want?" Thorne said.

I pushed my plate away.

"I don't know what I want," I said.

Thorne shrugged and swirled his pancake around in the yellow egg goo.

"We can wait," he said. "If you're determined to wuss out on me, we can stall for a couple days. Give you some time to think about Wailer doing the nasty with Luna Hayes, and Posie not even knowing."

"I don't want to think about that!" I said.

"Then what?"

"Just don't do anything yet, okay?" I made him promise. "Give me some time."

"Okay," Thorne said. He started singing some pirate song. "'Way hey, blow the man down. Give me some time to blow the man down.'"

I chewed the ice in my glass. "What does that mean, anyway, 'Blow the man down'? What is that?" I said.

"Beats me," Thorne said. "You know all those pirates were a little nuts. All those months at sea without any girls."

"You think?" I said.

---■---

I looked out the window at Thorne's car and thought about all the stuff we'd recorded. Wailer and Luna were probably still out on the dune together.

I didn't know what to do. I never do, I'm pathetic.

Oct. 8

I went to the mall today to get Honey a birthday present. Normally I wouldn't give it that much thought, but this one seems like a big deal to Honey, and I have a feeling I'm the only person she's going to get a present from. It's hard to shop for people, though. I wanted to get Honey just the right thing but I didn't know what.

Then I found this store called Ha Ha What's So Funny? which is full of all these jokes and novelties and some of them seemed like they'd crack my sister up. There was this soap which, the more you used it, the dirtier it turned your hands, and there was a fart pillow and all kinds of fake dog poop. I looked at the fake dog poop for a while, trying to choose between large, medium, and small, but somehow it didn't seem right. Close, but not perfect.

Then I saw this thing that you hook onto the back of your door, and if you open the door, this voice says, "Hey, stay the hell out of my room!" And next to that was a mirror, and if you look in the mirror, this voice starts to scream. They were so good that I decided to get them both. I even bought some nice paper at a drugstore so I could wrap them up later.

I was on my way out of the mall when guess who I saw, hanging out at the Bon Jon Surf Shop? Wailer and Luna. They were holding hands. They didn't see me, and I got the hell out of there as fast as I could. But it made me remember that I still have to decide what to do.

Maybe I should go back and get some of that fake dog poop for Wailer and put it in front of his locker. Except large isn't big enough for him.

—— ■ ——

I'm sitting in history class listening to Miss Tenuda talk about the Articles of Confederation. I kind of like Miss Tenuda. She's really short and squat, like a female Danny DeVito. I always expect her to suddenly drop down and start wrestling people. It would be great if she came to class one time in like, tights and a cape.

I appear to be taking very good notes right now. The only other person who is writing as furiously as I am is this girl in front of me named Rosa. She has fine black hair all over her arms which you'd think would be ugly, but I like it. Her lips are pink and full and her eyes stick out of her head like cue balls, with curly black lashes. When she moves, this odor of laundry detergent and coconut oil wafts into the air. All I want is to lie with Rosa underneath a palm tree on a deserted island and drink coconut milk right out of the coconut. We'll smoke cigars together and watch the smoke rings float one after the other, into the blue sky above the ocean.

Rosa just turned around and gave me a look, as if to say, "Stop writing about me." Now I'm sitting here staring at the back of her shirt. She's wearing a white T-shirt and I can see her bra through it. Her black hair comes down almost to the level of her bra in the back and it is very shiny, almost wet-looking. She has stopped writing again, as if she can tell I'm still writing about her and it's driving her crazy. I don't believe in ESP or any of that *X-Files* stuff, but sometimes I'm sure people can tell what you're thinking. Rosa knows I'm scanning her. It is sort of annoying her, but she sort of likes it, too.

For a moment my hand just hovers above her hair and I can feel the warmth and the electricity coming off of it. Then I lower my fingers and feel the coarse silkiness of it. Sophie isn't moving. I am wondering how long I can do this before Miss Tenuda notices. She seems pretty committed to the Articles of Confederation right now. Sophie turns around again and gives me this fierce look. "Jonah, what are you thinking about?" she asks me. "It's me, isn't it?"

Sophie is wearing a purple sarong over her bikini. She looks very tropical. We push off from shore on a wooden raft, and overhead the stars are shining. Sophie plays her mandolin and I unscrew the cap from a bottle of wine that is marked SERVE VERY COLD. I drink some and lean over Sophie and kiss her and she drinks the wine from my mouth. One of my hands is cupping her head, and I let the other hand fall into the river, which is warm and dark.

The two of us float downstream beneath the stars and from the shore we can hear the distant sounds of civilization, but we have no interest in ever going back to those bastards. Our hope is that we will wash up on the shores of a new nation together and live in the nude which we won't be ashamed of and we will eat the fruit from the trees. We will sit around the fire, and Sophie will play the mandolin and I will sing and we'll watch the smoke rise up to heaven.

Our children will form a new nation here, and in time they will come to believe that a federal form of government is the best way to serve the needs of the people. In 1780 they will form the second constitutional convention and draw up a document outlining the structure of the new federal government and its three parts: 1) executive, 2) legislative, 3) judiciary. The document will be amended on occasion and the first ten amendments to the Constitution will collectively be known as the Bill of

Okay, now I'm back after a very unpleasant moment. Miss Tenuda asked a question that no one knew the answer to, so she asked me to answer it because I've had all this stuff before. Except I didn't hear her because I was writing the little story above and she kept calling on me and I must have been pretty far out of it because I didn't hear her and she came all the way over to my desk and stood behind me reading what I was writing until finally I snapped out of it because Rosa turned around and looked at me again.

Then Miss Tenuda picks me up and spins me around and around over her head. And then she slams me down on the mat and the referees are blowing their whistles and the crowd is booing. But Miss Tenuda cannot be stopped and now she is pulling back my arms with some moves that are not sanctioned by the WWF.

"Jonah, I'd like to talk to you after class," she said.

So now I'm sitting here waiting for class to end so she can yell at me.

The funny thing is, when she asked me to stay after class, it didn't sound all that threatening. It sounded like she really wanted to talk to me.

I'm just about to head over to First Amendment for work but I wanted to write about my meeting with Miss Tenuda, which went really well.

Okay. After class everybody else cleared out of the room and she walked over to my desk and sat down in front of me.

"Listen, Miss Tenuda," I said. "I'm sorry I was daydreaming in class. But you know I studied all this last year."

"It's all right, Jonah. But I would appreciate it if you'd at least pretend to pay attention. It's rude of you to totally ignore what I'm saying."

"I'm sorry. I didn't mean to—"

"You don't have to apologize, Jonah. Actually, I want to talk to you about something else."

"About what?"

"Well, Dr. Chamberlin and I have been discussing your situation."

It was amazing! The first confirmed evidence that Dr. Chamberlin actually exists. I was imagining Miss Tenuda talking to the principal, sitting on the couch in the faculty lounge, smoking cigarettes, looking up at the ceiling, and saying, "Dr. Chamberlin? It's about this Jonah Black. . . ." And there is Dr. Chamberlin, who has a head five times the size of a normal human. It's got bulging veins that twitch. No wonder Dr. Chamberlin doesn't let anyone see him. It'd be too much of a shock.

"Yes," Miss Tenuda said. "We think it was a bit harsh for Masthead to have expelled you. It seems like a waste of your intelligence for you to be sitting here in eleventh grade all over again."

I sat up. I couldn't believe it. "You mean I can be a senior?"

"Not so fast. We can't just jump you up a grade now that the school year's begun. We need you to help us make the case to Mrs. Perella."

"Mrs. Perella?" I said. "But I mean—Dr. Chamberlin's the principal. Can't he just tell her what to do?"

Miss Tenuda smiled at me, like, it's clear you don't understand how the administration works. I guess even Dr. Chamberlin is afraid of Mrs. Perella.

"What do I have to do? I'll do anything," I said.

"I need you to get straight As this marking period. In all your subjects. Including German. Miss von Esse thinks that will be a particular challenge for you," Miss Tenuda said. "Do you think you can do it?"

"I think so," I said, although getting straight As wasn't going to be easy even if I did have all these classes last year.

"If you can get straight As, I think we can get Mrs. Perella to let you back in the senior class after the first marking period."

"Yes!" I said. "I'll definitely do it!" I couldn't believe it. Maybe there actually is a God.

She stood up. "And you'll pay attention in class?" Miss Tenuda said. "I can't give you an A if you're off in your own little world."

I rush forward and tackle her at the knees. Then I spin her around over my head and slap her down on the mat in a full body slam. The referees raise my hand in the air and the bell rings and everybody cheers!

"Yes," I said. "I'll pay attention."

"I don't want to see you writing a little story about, um . . ." she stammered. "Other members of the class."

"I promise."

I headed for the door. I could feel Miss Tenuda watching me. "You know, Jonah," she called after me. "If you become a senior, and leave this class . . ."

I stopped and turned around. "Yes?"

———— ■ ————

"Well. I'm going to miss you," she said.

She comes over to where I'm standing and hands me a towel. She makes a muscle with her bicep that is thicker than my thigh. There's oil dripping off it. I take the towel from her sweaty hand and wipe my face with it.

"I'll miss you, too," I said.

Oct. 10

I went online to see if I could chat with Northgirl but she wasn't on, so I just sat there wondering about her. Suddenly I had this huge insight—Northgirl is Watches Boys Dive! She's some local girl who doesn't go to Don Shula, probably. Maybe she's really shy. That's why she keeps disappearing, and why she's hiding her identity.

I don't know, the more I write this, the dumber it sounds. Maybe neither of them exists. That seems to be the kind of girl I do best with.

I wanted to talk to Posie about this. But then I've barely talked to Posie in the last week. I guess I'm kind of avoiding her because I can't handle seeing her together with Wailer. I wish I could show her the pictures Thorne and I took in a dream or something so she could just wake up and *know* what a slimeball Wailer is.

Oct. 11

Well, here it is the night before Honey's birthday and I can tell Honey is feeling pretty down about things because she's in her room with the door locked. Maybe I should give her her presents now. I have this terrible feeling that Mom's forgotten Honey's birthday, too. I think I'm going to say something tomorrow to make sure she's got something planned.

Until about five minutes ago Honey was listening to Hole, blasting it at top volume. Now she's got Mom's radio show on. I can never get used to people calling Mom to talk about their sex lives for all of Florida to listen. What makes it even worse is that every five minutes she stops and promotes her book, so in addition to all the bizarre conversations it's like this big infomercial. It gives me the creeps.

"Hello, you're on *Pillow Talk*!"

"Dr. Black, is it normal for a boy to masturbate three or four times a day?"

"I am so glad you asked that, caller! The important thing is that we all find our own levels of comfort. For some people three or four times a day might seem like a lot, but for others it's perfectly normal. You have to accept yourself for the person that you are and be nice to yourself. That's my real question, caller, Are you being nice to yourself?"

"I think so, Dr. Black. I guess what I want to know is if there's such a thing as being too nice to yourself."

"Too nice? I don't think so, caller!"

"Well, what if a person was doing it maybe five or six times a day? Would that be normal?"

"Caller, even five or six times a day is all right if the person feels good about themselves. For some persons this might feel right, but others might feel like it's starting to take time away from other things that are important. The real question is, Are you being nice to yourself?"

"How about seven or eight? Nine, sometimes?"

Hello? I'm trying to study for the German test tomorrow, but with this going on in the background it's a little hard to concentrate. Okay, in five minutes I will start to study, and I won't stop until I fall asleep.

I can't believe Dad still hasn't called Honey to wish her happy birthday. What an idiot.

I have to ace this test.

German stinks. It's like, the more I study the worse I get. Thorne has this whole theory of "negative knowledge," like there's a certain "optimum studying" period you can work on anything, and beyond that you start getting stupider. In Thorne's case the optimum studying period for everything lasts about seven minutes.

If I don't get at least an A minus on this, though, I'm going to be stuck in eleventh grade for the entire year. Unless the governor writes back and gives me a pardon, which I'm not exactly counting on.

Honey just got up and went out to the kitchen and opened the front door. But she didn't go out. She just closed the door and locked it and went back to her room where Mom's show is still playing. I wonder what she's up to.

Now there's a second source of noise on in her room, some kind of spoken-word tape, probably for one of her eighty different language classes. I hate how easy learning things is for her. She's learning Russian now, not at school, just all on her own.

She's laughing to herself, so she must have just said something really funny in Russian. *More vodka?*

Yes, thank you! Or maybe Mom said something funny I didn't hear.

What am I doing? I really hav

Okay, I'm back. Posie was just here. Things are not good.

In her usual style, Posie just appeared while I was sitting here, writing.

"What are you doing here?" I said. Really surprised. But I was nervous, too. Now that she was there, right in front of me, it was about time I told her about Wailer.

"I came to ask your advice about something," Posie said. "Can I come in?"

She walked in anyway, before I could answer, and sat down on the end of my bed. She was wearing a sleeveless shirt, and there were goose bumps on her arms. I didn't want her to leave, but I forced myself to say that I did.

"I don't know. Now's not the best time, Posie," I said.

"It isn't?" She punched me. "Hel-*lo*? Jonah? It's *me*."

"I'm supposed to be studying German. I have a test tomorrow and if I don't get an A I'm going to have to stay in eleventh grade," I explained.

"But I need to talk, Jonah. Please?" she said. "I promise it won't take too long."

What could I do? I sat down next to her and she took my hand.

"Listen. I wanted to ask your opinion about something," she said.

I could still hear Honey talking in Russian in the next room. Her tape was getting louder. Or maybe it was the radio. "I like small beds," a male voice said. Honey giggled.

"About what?" I asked Posie.

"About Wailer," she said, squeezing my hand and smiling as she said it.

Oh, no, I thought. "What about him?"

"Do you think he loves me? I mean really?" she asked.

My heart started beating like crazy. Was Posie beginning to wonder if Wailer was for real? I knew I had to say something.

From the next room came more giggling. I realized then that Honey had someone in there with her. She had gone out to the kitchen before to let someone in.

"Hey, do you want to take a walk or something?" I asked Posie.

"No, I want you to tell me what you really think."

"About what?" I said, stalling.

"About Wailer."

I took a deep breath.

"Posie," I said. "There's something you should know."

Now there was hysterical laughter from the other side of the wall, and this time it was clear that the tape I thought she was listening to wasn't a tape at all. It was the voice of some guy.

"I want to get married!" Honey shouted, like this was the funniest thing in the world.

Honey and her friend both shrieked at this. The guy grunted, and suddenly I recognized that grunt.

"I want to have babies!" he said.

"We can live on the beach!" squealed Honey, like this was the funniest joke ever told.

"I'll teach you how to surf!" said Wailer.

Posie stood up. She looked at the wall, then at me. Her face was stony, her eyes wide.

"Is that—?"

Wailer's laugh rang out clearly. Honey giggled some more.

Posie hugged herself, tears streaking her face. I stood up to hold her but she slapped my hand away.

"Why, Jonah?" She sobbed. "Why would you do this to me?" she said.

"But Posie," I said. "I didn't know he was there. I didn't know—"

"Liar," Posie said.

It was the meanest thing she'd ever said to me. But I realized that in a way I had lied to her.

"You're supposed to be my friend," Posie said quietly, her voice all broken. And then she ran outside and down to the dock.

I started to go after her, but by the time I got there her motorboat was already a ways down Cocoabutter Creek.

"Posie!" I called. "Damn."

I stood there in the backyard thinking about going after her on my bike. Then I remembered the German test. I had to go back and study. If I didn't, I was a dead man. I looked back at the house. Goddamned Honey.

So here I am, about to start studying, while Posie is out on the water somewhere, in tears.

Oct. 12

Honey's birthday. I just took the German test, and I think I screwed it up. Now I'm in study hall writing this.

The reason I screwed up the test is everything that happened last night. Which was this:

After Posie left I tried studying for a while but it was impossible. Just to kill some time while my head stopped swimming, I tried to go online with Northgirl. But all I got was "Northgirl999 is not currently signed on."

I heard Wailer leave. A little after that, Honey came into my room. She was wearing a big football jersey that went down to her knees. A gift from the football team, I guess.

"Okay, Elmo," Honey said. "Now's your chance. She's all ready for you."

"What are you talking about?"

"Your friend. Posie. She's yours," Honey said.

"What do you mean she's mine?" I said.

"I guarantee you, Jonah," Honey said, with her hands on her hips. "You find her right now, she'll do anything you want. Trust me."

I stared at her. And then it dawned on me. This was Honey's big scheme.

"You *planned* this?" I said, outraged.

"I told you I was going to get you something you needed," Honey said, looking very pleased with herself.

"I don't know what you're talking about," I said. "Posie's my friend." Even as I said it I knew I sounded like a broken record.

"You," Honey growled, "are such a loser!" She started to leave my room.

"Wait," I said, stopping her. "Why did you do this, anyway? What do you care who I go out with?"

"I don't know, Brotherman. Maybe I'm hoping you'll do something nice for me once in a while."

That's when I remembered the presents I'd bought her. I got them out of my closet and gave them to her. She lit a cigarette and unwrapped them.

"I'm saving the paper," she said. She examined the presents—the thing for the door that said, "Hey, stay the hell out of my room," and the mirror that screamed—and nodded appreciatively.

"Nice," she said, and gave me a hug. "Thanks."

I just shrugged like it was nothing, but secretly I was pleased that she liked them.

"Okay," she said. "I'm heading out."

"Now?"

"Of course now. That's the nice thing about having a mother with a live radio show. You always know where she is." She went back to her room to change and then she drove off in her Jeep.

At that moment, the phone began to ring. On the radio, I could still hear Mom talking. "The female orgasm helps a woman release all her body stress. The female orgasm is a miracle!"

The phone was still ringing, so I picked it up.

"Hello? Jonah?"

"Who's this?" I said, although I knew perfectly well who it was.

"It's your dad, Jonah. Your dad!"

"Hi."

"Got your message, son. Glad you reminded me. Would have forgotten. Is your sister there?"

"No, Dad," I said. "You missed her."

I talked to Dad for about a minute. He said he's doing well. Tiffany just won first prize in the Sugartown Horse Show. Now they're going to Switzerland for a week. She likes to ski. It's like he was calling from another dimension.

By then it was almost nine o'clock. I had about two more hours of German if I expected to even pass the test, let alone get an A. But maybe Honey was right, I thought. Maybe I should go find Posie. She was out there somewhere, probably crying her heart out. But if I went to look for her I'd fail my test, which meant I'd have to stay in eleventh grade, and then Posie would graduate at the end of the year and go off somewhere to college and leave me behind.

I tried to clear my mind. I sat down at my desk and looked at the list of all the vocabulary words I was supposed to memorize.

But I just kept hearing what Posie had said. *You're supposed to be my friend.*

Was that all I wanted, to be her friend?

On the radio, Mom said, "Multiple sex partners for the female? Perfectly natural, if you're comfortable with it. The question is, are you being nice to yourself?"

(Still Oct. 12, later.)

Now I'm in Miss Tenuda's class, still trying to catch up on the gory details of last night. I have to make sure she doesn't see me writing this instead of taking notes or she's going to get ticked off and maybe not let me be a senior even if I do, by some miracle, get an A on that German test.

Anyway, it didn't take me very long last night to decide to go after Posie. She was more important than any stupid German test, even more important than me being a senior. It wasn't even a hard decision to make. I just got up and went outside and got on my bike and rode over to her house.

As I rode I thought about how long I'd known Posie. I remembered how her father had this old bull whip and we'd stand in her driveway, trying to crack it, scaring the dog. I remembered her teaching me how to chew tobacco. And watching her shoot a perfect basket from midcourt when she was only twelve. I thought about her in that red bikini top she left on the floor of my room. And then I started thinking that even if I went over there and said stupid things and made a complete ass of myself, Posie wouldn't mind. She'd be okay about it. That kind of gave me courage.

Finally I got to her house. I didn't want to disturb her parents so I opened the front door without knocking and crept up the back stairs to her room. Posie's little sister, Caitlin, was lying on her bed with her headphones on. The door to Posie's room was closed, but the light was on.

I knocked softly. "Posie? It's me, Jonah," I said.

I heard a kind of gasp from inside. It sounded like she was still crying. So I opened the door slowly.

Sitting on the bed were Posie and Thorne, with their arms wrapped around each other.

"Oh, Thorne," Posie said, leaning against Thorne. "Look. Jonah's here."

Thorne just nodded at me. I didn't know what to think. I was so pissed at him for being there, but even more mad at myself. I mean if I'd just gotten there a little sooner, I could have been the one with my arms around Posie. I'm such an idiot.

Thorne kissed Posie's hair and stood up. "I have to head out," he said.

"No, stay," Posie said, grabbing his hand.

"Yeah, Thorne," I said hollowly. "Stay."

But Thorne shook his head. "Sorry," he said. "I'll call you in the morning, Pose."

Then he kind of shoved passed me in the doorway without meeting my gaze. I turned back to Posie. Her face was all blotchy like she'd been crying for a while, but she looked okay, much better than she had at my house.

"What the hell was that all about?" I said.

"Oh, Jonah," Posie said. "Don't be angry. Thorne was great. He said all the right things."

"I thought you said Thorne brings you down. All

he ever wants to talk about is sex, you said," I accused her jealously.

"Yeah, well, Thorne's a pretty sensitive guy underneath that whole act of his. He's always looking out for me," Posie said. "He's a real sweetie."

"I'm always looking out for you, too," I said, lamely.

"I know," Posie said, smiling up at me. "I'm so lucky to have you guys."

But that wasn't enough for me. Something about the way Thorne had kissed her hair just seemed so familiar and intimate. I felt like something had happened. Something I'd missed out on.

"So are you and Thorne like, together now?" I said.

Posie blushed deep purple. I couldn't believe it!

"No," she stammered. "I don't know. I think—I think we're going to take it slowly."

"Okay," I said, exasperated. "Fine. Listen, I just wanted to say—"

"It's all right, Jonah," Posie said. She stood up and blew her nose. "I'm not mad at you anymore. I should never have listened to Wailer. I just wanted to believe all his bullshit, you know?"

My heart kind of sank when she said that. I mean, why did she have to believe anyone's bullshit—Wailer's, or Thorne's—when I was standing right there in front of her, ready to tell her the truth?

"It's okay," I said.

I went over and kissed her on the cheek and looked into her eyes for a second. For the first time ever I felt like I didn't know what she was thinking, and she definitely didn't know what I was thinking. Her old stuffed bear was on her bed—Mr. Tummy, he's called. I picked him up and tucked him under the covers. Then I left before I could say anything stupid.

(Still Oct. 12, midnight.)

Mom forgot Honey's birthday completely. She went out with someone for dinner and didn't come home until late. Honey acted like she didn't even notice. I picked up a ham and pineapple pizza from First Amendment and took out *Repo Man*. She loves that movie. So we sat on the floor in the living room and ate and watched the movie and then I did some dives for her out in the pool. I hope she had a good birthday.

Oct. 15

We got the German tests back. B minus. Scheiss.
I'm a junior.

I'm waiting to go in and see Dr. LaRue. The girl
who's always here in the waiting room is here again.
But she looks different today. She's wearing makeup.
She seems like a different person.

She says, "Are you okay?"

And I say, "No, I'm not okay. I think I'm beginning to realize how not okay I am."

"It's all right," she says. "A lot of people are
nuts. That doesn't make them bad. Or undesir-
able."

She comes over and sits next to me and takes
my hand. "My mother is all upset because I like to
do it with guys I hardly even know," she says.

"Is that why you're in therapy?" I say.

"No, that's why *she's* in therapy. I'm fine with it.

216

I like guys. They're all so different," she says. "It's like some guys are warriors and some are kings and some are lovers and others are mystics."

And some guys are big liars, I think to myself.

And then she says, "What do you think you are, Jonah Black?"

"I don't know what I am," I tell her.

"I do," she says. "You're a lover."

And then she climbs into my lap, and, just as our lips meet, she says, "That's my favorite kind."

"Jonah?"

That's my name.

Dr. LaRue is calling me in. More later.

(Still Oct. 16, 11 P.M.)

My fourth session with Dr. LaRue was interesting. I have to say I'm beginning to hate going to him a little less. Not because I think he knows anything, or because I think he can do anything for me, but because it's good to have someone to talk to. Even if he does look like one of the Muppets and I can always hear the drill from the dentist next door.

We spent the first half of the session talking about Mom and Dad's divorce, and I answered all his questions without making a single thing up. I think I'm too tired to keep making up stories for him. Anyway, I've fed him enough bullshit so that even when I tell him the truth now he probably won't believe me.

At the end of the session he started asking me about Posie, which was funny because I don't even remember telling him about Posie.

"Who's a better friend to you, Posie or Thorne?"

"I don't know. They're different. You relate differently to your guy friends and your girl friends."

"A lot of boys your age don't have girls for friends. Do you think you're unusual having a close friend who's a girl?"

"I don't know if I'm unusual or not," I said. I thought it was a pretty dumb question. I mean nobody walks around thinking about how unusual they are, do they?

"Well, I think you are unusual, Jonah," Dr. LaRue said. "I talk to a lot of young people, every day. They come in here and they complain about their friends. You don't do that, Jonah. Why do you think that is?"

"I don't know."

"I think it's because you're loyal. And you put other people's needs before your own."

"I guess," I said. It sounded like he was just repeating stuff from last time.

"Do you think it's silly, for a person to act that way?"

"What way?" I said.

"Putting other people's needs ahead of their own."

"Yeah. I guess. I mean, it's a good thing to do," I said, thinking about it. "But it can hurt you."

"Is that what happened at Masthead? Did you get hurt because you were looking out for Sophie O'Brien instead of yourself?"

I thought about this a long time. I wasn't sure how to explain what had happened. And I wasn't sure I was ready.

"That might have been part of it," I said. "That, and bad luck. I mean, what happened at Masthead was really an accident."

"What part of it was an accident?"

I kind of smiled, even though I didn't think it was all that funny. "Well, the part of it that was an actual accident was an accident."

"What do you mean, an actual accident?"

"The part where I drove the car through the motel wall was an accident."

I heard Dr. LaRue's pencil scratching against his yellow pad. He was writing down a lot now. From next door I heard the whine of the dentist's drill.

"What do you think . . ." Dr. LaRue said, and paused. He was trying to choose his words carefully. "What effect did this car accident have on you?"

I thought for a long time. I thought about getting thrown out of school, and leaving Dad's house, and moving back in with Mom and Honey, and having to repeat eleventh grade.

"The most important effect it had on me?" I said.

"Yes."

"I lost my driver's license."

Dr. LaRue sighed, like this was the wrong answer. I don't know, maybe it was the wrong answer, but maybe it's not. I think the fact that I can't drive is a huge thing. It totally sucks. Even if I were a senior, I'd still be riding my bike around Pompano Beach like a little kid.

"All right," Dr. LaRue said. It sounded like he'd given up. "I think that's enough for today."

—— ■ ——

I'm sitting here at First Amendment Pizza, waiting for the pizza to cook so I can deliver it. Oh, the Swedes are all happy again, giving each other little kisses and smiling, like they just started going out or something. It's strange how people can hate each other one week and then be kissing the back of each other's necks the next.

I talked to Thorne today in the weight room. I'm doing this really hard-core workout these days, because our first meet is tomorrow. Anyway, I'd nearly finished my routine—bench press, bicep curls, tricep curls, lateral pulldowns, leg curls, leg extensions, and squats—when Thorne came over and sat down on the bench next to me.

We hadn't talked since I saw him at Posie's house, and I'm still kind of pissed at him. I think he knows this.

Anyway, he handed me a piece of paper.

"What's this?" I said.

Then I looked down and saw the words—*Sophie O'Brien. 17 Hemlock Point. Kennebunkport, ME 04906. (207) 555-8749.*

"Jesus, Thorne. You found her."

I couldn't believe it. I stared at the printout. My forehead went cold.

"Yeah, and it wasn't easy, either. I think her father is CIA or something, man. The address is totally unlisted. It was like trying to uncover a state secret. I mean, what's the story with this chick, anyway? You ever going to tell me?"

I wasn't even listening to him. I was thinking about how fall break was soon. Masthead would close for a week and everybody would go back to their parents' houses. I imagined the phone ringing in her house. Sophie picks it up. Her father looks at her suspiciously.

"Hello? Sophie? I'm not sure you remember me? But my name is Jonah Black, and—"

"Hello?" Thorne said.

"I don't want to talk about it," I said.

"Yeah, well, listen, Jonah, I'm getting kind of

tired of this 'I don't want to talk about it' thing. Are you and me friends or what?" he said.

I took a moment to think this over. I think Thorne giving me Sophie's address was his way of making it up to me for being all cuddly with Posie when he knew I was the one who wanted to be with her. I didn't completely forgive him. But no matter what kind of crap he pulls, I feel like I'm stuck with Thorne, the same way you're stuck with your family.

"Yeah," I said. "We're friends."

"So you better tell me about this Sophie then, because it's pissing me off," Thorne said.

"It's hard for me to talk about, all right?" I said, getting irritated. It was like someone getting in your face and saying, "Tell me right now how you feel about your dad dying. Come on, tell me!" or some such bullshit. It really wasn't right.

"Okay," Thorne said. "You don't have to tell me right this second. But sometime soon, all right? I mean, you're making me feel like an idiot."

"Thorne?" I said.

"Yeah?"

"You *are* an idiot."

Thorne laughed. He looked relieved, like he'd really been worried that I was mad at him.

I put the piece of paper in my pocket. I felt like

I'd just put a check in there for a huge amount of money. I was already worried about losing it.

"I'll tell you about it sometime. I promise," I said.

Thorne slapped me on the shoulder. "Okay. And maybe I'll tell you some of my secrets sometime."

I don't know what he meant by that, and guess what? I don't want to know.

(Still Oct. 17, 9:15 P.M.)

I'm back in my room with a pile of homework that is not worth doing anymore. I think I can probably coast through this whole year now and get Bs without trying too hard. I'm not feeling especially motivated. It's just too depressing.

When I got back home, Mom was sitting at the kitchen table looking like she'd just swallowed the canary. She's going on a six-week national tour, she said, to plug *Pillow Talk* as well as *Hello Penis! Hello Vagina!* While she's away Honey and I are going to be on our own, and she wanted to know if we can accept the responsibility. In particular she wants to know if I'll look out for Honey.

"Honey doesn't need looking out for," I said. "She looks out for herself."

"Well, you've seen her, locked in that room of

224

hers," Mom said, filing her nails with an emery board. "She studies too much. She needs to get out and have a little fun."

She wasn't even kidding. What about Honey roaring off in her Jeep at all hours of the night to visit the football team, or Smacky Platte? I guess Mom really and truly believes that Honey is helping them study. She probably thinks Honey studies all the time. I guess it would be hard to understand your daughter, who skips grades without even trying, if you had a son who was repeating grades and failing them.

"You're right, Mom," was all I said.

She kept filing her nails until her cell phone rang.

"Hello?" she said. She pulled her Palm Pilot out of her purse. "Well, I'm sure we can get together while I'm on tour. Haven't you been talking about going to New York?" she said, her voice all girly. She covered the receiver with her hand, "I have to take this," she told me. And then she got up and walked into her bedroom.

(Still Oct. 17, midnight.)

I was just wondering if I should burn this journal like I burned the others. I mean what am I writing this all down for anyway? I'm certainly not going to want to look back on all these days in my life. They're too pathetic.

I spent a lot of the night just sitting on my bed looking at Sophie's address and phone number. I picked up the phone once, listened to the dial tone, and dialed all except for the last number. I just looked at my finger, knowing I could push that button, and talk to her. But I couldn't do it.

So I went over to see Posie instead. I had to talk to someone. So I climbed on my bike and headed over there.

But then, parked in front of Posie's house, there was Thorne's VW Beetle. I decided not to go inside.

So now I'm back in my room, trying to get a grip. I just got off the Internet. I was trying to IM Northgirl. But now AOL says Northgirl999 is not a valid username. I don't get it.

Maybe I should read *Hello Penis! Hello Vagina!* Maybe it really does have all the answers. Or maybe I should just tie it to my leg and jump in the pool and let myself sink.

Oct. 18

Today was the first preseason swim meet of the year. Don Shula's team kind of stinks, and Wailer and Martino and I were the only divers. But we gave it our best shot. We were competing against Fran Tarkington High School in Ft. Lauderdale, and those guys really have a squad, like six guys doing diving alone.

It was the first time I'd seen Wailer since the blowup with Posie. I tried to talk to him about it before the meet, but he just waved me off and said something about needing to focus. I let it go. And actually, he was right. Coach Davis would be furious if he knew I was trying to have it out with Wailer right before the meet. Besides, what was there to say?

We got into the pool and did our warm-ups and then we got out and waited around for the meet to start. While I was waiting I looked up at the crowd in the stands. For a preseason meet the place was pretty packed. Some of my teachers were there, like Miss von Esse, and Mrs. Perella, and Miss Tenuda, and Mr. Bond. A man in a wheelchair with an oxygen mask strapped over his face was sitting next to Miss Tenuda, and I wondered if maybe he was our principal, Dr. Chamberlin. Maybe he was very sick and that's why we never saw him.

Thorne was sitting with his arm around Posie. She looked so beautiful and I could almost smell her hair just by looking at it. We made eye contact and she smiled at me and waved. I held up my hand to wave, and Mr. Davis looked up at her and then at me and I knew he was worrying whether or not some girl was going to make me lose my concentration.

In the row in front of Thorne and Posie were all these girls I knew. Cecily LaChoy and Shanique O'Reilly. Cheese Girl, sitting by herself. Rosa was sitting with this huge guy who goes to Ely High School. Luna Hayes. Dell Merriwether. Even Posie's little sister, Caitlin, was there.

An old man was sitting all alone in the top row. It was Pops Berman, wearing a black windbreaker and his Red Sox hat. I had almost forgotten about him.

Honey was sitting off in a corner near the back, surrounded by the guys from the football team.

The only people missing who I would've wanted there were Mom and Sophie. And Watches Boys Dive. I looked all around for her, but she wasn't there. I missed her. It made me nervous, her disappearing like that.

Mom wasn't there because she was in Pittsburgh, doing a morning talk show and signing books at a Waldenbooks in some mall. *Hello Penis!* is on the "Top Bestsellers of the Year" list of the *South Florida Sun-Sentinel.* Unbelievable.

And Sophie wasn't there because she had no reason to be there. She was probably just arriving back at her family's house in Kennebunkport, Maine, for fall break. I already had her phone number memorized, and I was trying to decide whether or not to call her. It was something I wanted to figure out before I did my dive.

The officials called me to the board. I had signed up to do a pretty straightforward dive, a double somersault. But all of a sudden I didn't want to do that dive anymore, I wanted to do something impressive.

So I'd decided to try the back two-and-a-half somersault with a one-and-a-half twist. The one Mr. Davis said not to do unless I was physically and mentally ready.

I felt ready.

The whole pool and the bleachers got really quiet as I walked out to the end of the board. Then Pops Berman growled out, "Go get 'em, Chipper!"

I wanted to look up at Pops but instead I just shut out the world. I stood at the edge of the board on my toes with my heels sticking out into empty space. It was so quiet, that same quiet of an orchestra just before the conductor raises his hand. All of a sudden I realized I was putting myself in real danger for no good reason. If I did the dive wrong my head could hit the board. I could even die. It wasn't a good thing to think at the time.

But I shut out the world and the only thing I could hear was my own heart. I pressed down on the board with the weight of my whole body, then I raised my arms up over my head and pushed off. In a moment I had left everything behind and was flying through the air. I did the somersaults, one, two, two and a half, and right at the apex of my dive I saw Sophie again.

We're riding horses on the beach near her family's place in Kennebunkport. The wind blows her long blond hair in her eyes and she pulls back

Angel's reins and we stop. The horses' legs are ankle-deep in water. We jump off and leave the horses standing there, and just leap into the surf. She's wearing her red bikini, but I've got all my clothes on. I can hear the thunder of the waves and feel the spray on my cheeks and Posie's eyes glow with the warm pink light of sunset.

"Come on, Jonah, let's go surfing," she says.

And I say, "I don't know how."

"I'll teach you," Posie says. "Don't worry, it's fun."

And I say, "I'm scared."

So she takes me by the hand and this big wave surges up and we dive beneath it. Now Posie and I are underwater and we are swimming like fish and diving deeper and deeper below the surface and there on the ocean floor below us is an amazing place—flickering sunlight and coral and schools of glowing fish and seaweed swaying in the current. The school of phosphorescent jellyfish is above us, glowing green and orange, and I can't believe we are finally here together in this beautiful place. And Posie says, without speaking, "It was down here all along."

And then I thought, *Posie? What's she doing here?*

Then I realized I have a choice to make. There's

Posie, my friend, who has always been there, who I love. And then there's Sophie, the girl I gave up everything for, my dream girl, who I also love in a different way. She's standing outside the train station on the day that I left Masthead wearing her yellow dress and red fishing hat and she's watching my train pull away. She raises one hand as if to stop the train, but it starts to move down the tracks. The wind knocks her hat off and she stands there with her blond hair blowing around in the sunshine.

How can I leave her behind?

I heard Coach Davis swear because at that exact second I lost my center of balance. If I didn't do the two-and-a-half twist exactly right while correcting for my mistake I was going to hit the board and break my neck.

I was operating in slow motion. I knew I was in trouble, but it was still possible that I could pull it off. A person is capable of all sorts of miracles. I think maybe believing in them is what makes these miracles possible.

I heard the crowd gasp as everyone realized something had gone wrong. All the while I was spinning and floating through space.

And suddenly I knew exactly what to do.

Above the crowd I thought I heard a girl's voice.

"Jonah!"

I closed my eyes. Something hurt, a lot, like I'd been struck in the neck with a harpoon. I was falling.

Then I was underwater, surrounded by mermaids and jellyfish and coral and light. The world seemed very far away.

I felt the sea floor beneath me, and I lay on my back on the bottom of the ocean like I was sleeping in my own bed. It was peaceful down there. I looked up at the distant light coming from the other world and wondered if I'd ever float back to the surface.

WILL JONAH CALL SOPHIE?
WHO IS NORTHGIRL999?
WILL JONAH EVER KISS POSIE?
AND WHY *WAS* JONAH EXPELLED
FROM BOARDING SCHOOL?

FIND OUT IN THE NEXT INSTALLMENT OF
JONAH BLACK'S JOURNAL . . .

The Black Book
[DIARY OF A TEENAGE STUD]

VOL. II: STOP, DON'T STOP